This is a work of fiction. Similarities to real people, places, or events are entirely coincidental.

ECLIPSED BY DESIRE

First edition. June 4, 2024.

Copyright © 2024 Ivap Lawarga.

ISBN: 979-8224192076

Written by Ivap Lawarga.

Eclipsed by Desire

- Untangling Love, Loss, and Renewal

Disclaimer

This book is a work of fiction. Names, characters, places, and incidents are either the product of the author's imagination or used fictitiously. Any resemblance to actual persons, living or dead, or actual events is purely coincidental.

The views and opinions expressed in this book are those of the characters and do not necessarily reflect the official policy or position of any agency of the author, publisher, or any other organization. The characters, events, and dialogues are used to enhance the narrative and should not be interpreted as factual representations or endorsements of real-life situations or behaviors.

The author has made every effort to ensure the accuracy and completeness of the information contained within the book; however, the author assumes no responsibility or liability for any errors, omissions, or inaccuracies. Any actions taken based on the information in this book are at the reader's own risk. This book may contain mature themes and is intended for adult readers. Reader discretion is advised.

All rights reserved. No part of this book may be reproduced, distributed, or transmitted in any form or by any means, including photocopying, recording, or other electronic or mechanical methods, without the prior written permission of the author, except in the case of brief quotations embodied in critical reviews and certain other noncommercial uses permitted by copyright law.

For permission requests, please contact the author.

Author

Ivap Lawarga is a prolific author whose works explore the intricate dynamics of human relationships, resilience, and personal growth. With a background in psychology and a keen understanding of the human spirit, Ivap weaves narratives that resonate deeply with readers, offering insights into the complexities of love, forgiveness, and the paths to healing.

Born and raised in a small town, Ivap developed a passion for storytelling at an early age, finding inspiration in the everyday lives of people around him. This keen observation of human behavior and emotions has become a hallmark of his writing, bringing characters to life in a way that feels both authentic and relatable.

Ivap's previous works have garnered critical acclaim for their emotional depth and engaging plots, making him a beloved author among readers who appreciate stories that reflect the trials and triumphs of real life.

In addition to writing, Ivap is an avid traveler and a passionate advocate for mental health awareness. He believes in the transformative power of stories to heal and connect people, and he often draws from his own experiences and observations to create rich, compelling narratives.

When he's not writing, Ivap enjoys spending time with his family, exploring nature, and engaging in thoughtful conversations with friends and readers. He currently resides in a charming cottage by the sea, where he continues to write stories that inspire and move readers around the world.

Join Ivap on his literary journey and discover the powerful, heartwarming stories that have touched the lives of so many.

Preface

In the journey of life, the paths we tread often lead us to unexpected destinations. We are shaped by the choices we make, the relationships we nurture, and the challenges we face. This story, set against the backdrop of everyday life, explores the intricacies of human emotions, the strength of family bonds, and the complexities of love and forgiveness.

James, Emily, and Max are a family striving to find their way through the tumultuous seas of betrayal and healing. Their story is one of resilience, reflecting the struggles and triumphs that many of us face in our own lives. James, torn between duty and desire, makes a decision that sends ripples through the lives of those he loves most. Emily, grappling with her own vulnerabilities, finds unexpected connections that challenge her understanding of love and loyalty. Max, caught in the crossfire, searches for stability and comfort in a world that seems to be falling apart.

Sarah, too, plays a pivotal role in this narrative, representing the complexities of human connection and the unintended consequences of our actions. Her relationship with James brings to light the delicate balance between longing and responsibility, forcing all involved to confront their deepest fears and desires.

This book is a testament to the human spirit's capacity for growth and redemption. It delves into the shadows of infidelity, the pain of betrayal, and the arduous process of rebuilding trust. It also highlights the unexpected beauty that can emerge from the most challenging circumstances, the new beginnings that await us when we dare to face our truths.

As you turn the pages, you will witness the characters' struggles, their moments of doubt, and their ultimate journey towards healing and forgiveness. This is a story about finding strength in vulnerability, about the power of love to mend what is broken, and about the hope that resides in every new dawn.

I invite you to join James, Emily, Max, and Sarah as they navigate the complexities of their intertwined lives. May their story inspire you to reflect on your own relationships, to embrace forgiveness, and to believe in the possibility of new beginnings, no matter how difficult the path may seem.

Thank you for embarking on this journey with us.

Sincerely,

Ivap

Chapter 0: Troubled Skies

The morning sun filtered through the thin curtains of the master bedroom, casting a muted glow over the room. James Carter, dressed in his crisp pilot's uniform, glanced at his reflection in the mirror. Dark circles under his eyes told the story of another sleepless night. Emily lay in bed, the covers pulled up to her chin, her back turned to him.

"Emily, I have an early flight today," James said, his voice barely masking his weariness.

Emily's response was a muffled grunt, her indifference palpable. She finally turned over, her eyes cold. "Another early flight. Another day you're gone."

James sighed, straightening his tie. "It's my job. You knew this when we got married."

Emily sat up, her silk nightgown rustling softly. "Your job, always your job. What about your family, James? What about us?"

Downstairs, Max sat at the kitchen table, his breakfast untouched. He wore his school uniform, a white shirt and navy blue pants, and his hair was disheveled. He could hear the tension in his parents' voices drifting down from upstairs.

James descended the stairs, the tension still clinging to him. He forced a smile for Max, ruffling his son's hair. "Morning, buddy."

Max looked up, his eyes reflecting a mixture of concern and resignation. "Morning, Dad. You and Mom fighting again?"

James' smile faltered. "Just... talking. Don't worry about it."

Emily appeared at the top of the stairs, her expression a mix of anger and frustration. "James, we need to finish this conversation."

James looked at her, then back at Max. "Max, eat your breakfast. I'll be right back."

In the hallway, the argument resumed. Emily's voice was low but heated. "You're never here, James. When you are, it's like you're somewhere else. I can't keep doing this."

James ran a hand through his hair. "I'm trying, Emily. I really am. But you're always so distant, so... cold."

Emily crossed her arms, her silk nightgown shimmering in the morning light. "Maybe if you were here more, things would be different."

The air between them was thick with unresolved anger and sadness. James could feel the weight of it pressing down on him. He glanced back at Max, who was now staring at his cereal, his appetite gone.

"Emily, I have to go. We'll talk more when I get back." James' voice was strained.

Emily turned away, her silence more cutting than any words she could have spoken. James kissed Max on the forehead, his heart aching for the normalcy they once had.

As James walked out the door, the cool morning air hit his face, a stark contrast to the suffocating atmosphere inside. He took a deep breath, trying to shake off the tension. His thoughts drifted to the conference he was attending later that day, unaware of how much it would change his life.

Inside, Emily sat down at the kitchen table, her eyes fixed on Max. "Finish your breakfast, honey. You'll be late for school."

Max nodded, picking up his spoon with a heavy sigh. The house felt colder, emptier without James. The unspoken words hung in the air, a constant reminder of the growing chasm between his parents.

THE FOLLOWING EVENING, the house was silent when James returned from his flight. He dropped his bag at the door and found Emily in the kitchen, angrily scrubbing a pot.

"Hi," he said, cautiously.

Emily didn't look up. "What do you want, James?"

"Can we talk?" he asked, his voice strained.

She slammed the pot down, water splashing onto the counter. "Talk? What's there to talk about? You're never here, and when you are, it's like you don't give a damn about us."

James felt his temper rising. "That's not fair, Emily. I'm working hard to provide for this family."

Emily spun around, her face flushed with anger. "Fair? You think it's fair that I'm stuck here doing everything while you're off flying around the world? Max barely sees you. Hell, I barely see you."

James clenched his fists, struggling to keep his voice down. "I'm doing my best. Maybe if you appreciated what I do, things would be different."

Emily's eyes flashed. "Appreciate? I'm sick of your excuses, James. You're nothing but a selfish bastard who puts his job before his family."

Max appeared in the doorway, his eyes wide. "Mom, Dad, please stop."

James and Emily both froze, the air thick with the echo of their shouting. Emily turned away, tears brimming in her eyes. James reached out to Max, his heart breaking.

"Go to your room, Max. We'll sort this out," James said softly.

Max hesitated, then nodded and left, his footsteps heavy on the stairs. James turned back to Emily, his anger replaced by exhaustion.

"This can't keep happening, Emily. We need to find a way to make this work."

Emily wiped her eyes, her voice cold. "Maybe it's too late for that, James. Maybe we're just too broken to fix."

James felt a lump in his throat as he watched her walk away, the weight of their broken relationship pressing down on him. He knew things had to change, but he had no idea how to start mending the pieces of their shattered lives.

Chapter 1: Reunion

The grand ballroom of the downtown hotel buzzed with the lively chatter of aviation professionals. Crystal chandeliers cast a warm, golden glow over the elegantly decorated room. James Carter, dressed in a tailored navy suit, scanned the room with a practiced eye. He felt a strange mix of excitement and weariness, the day's events still fresh in his mind.

He adjusted his tie and stepped further into the crowd, exchanging polite nods and handshakes. The conference was in full swing, and he found himself surrounded by familiar faces. His thoughts drifted to the argument with Emily that morning, a dull ache settling in his chest.

A sudden, familiar laugh caught his attention. His heart skipped a beat. He turned, and there she was. Sarah Walker, his ex-girlfriend from nearly two decades ago, stood by the bar, a glass of wine in her hand. She wore a sleek, black dress that hugged her curves, her auburn hair cascading over her shoulders. She hadn't changed a bit.

"Sarah?" he called out, his voice tinged with disbelief.

She looked up, her eyes widening in recognition. "James! Oh my god, it's been ages!"

They moved towards each other, the crowd around them fading into the background. James felt a rush of emotions – shock, nostalgia, excitement. He had imagined this moment so many times, but reality surpassed his wildest dreams.

"How have you been?" he asked, his voice a mix of amazement and joy.

Sarah smiled, her eyes twinkling. "I've been good. Busy with work, you know how it is. And you? Still flying high, I see."

James chuckled, the sound of her voice bringing back a flood of memories. "Yeah, still at it. It's great to see you, really."

They found a quiet corner of the room, away from the noise and clinking glasses. The soft murmur of the crowd provided a backdrop as they caught up on lost years. Sarah spoke about her career, her travels, the ups and downs of life. James listened intently, his eyes never leaving her face.

"You look... amazing, Sarah," he said, his voice sincere. "I can't believe it's been eighteen years."

Sarah laughed softly, a hint of sadness in her eyes. "Time flies, doesn't it? You haven't changed much either, James. Still the same old you."

James felt a pang of regret, memories of their breakup surfacing. "I've missed you, you know. I always wondered what happened to you."

Sarah's smile faltered for a moment, a shadow passing over her features. "I missed you too, James. Life just... took us in different directions."

They fell silent, the weight of unspoken words hanging between them. James reached out, taking her hand in his. The touch was electric, sending a jolt through him. Sarah's eyes met his, a spark of something old and familiar reigniting.

"Remember that summer we spent at the lake?" James asked, a wistful smile spreading across his face.

Sarah's eyes lit up with the memory. "How could I forget? Those were some of the best days of my life. We used to sneak out early in the morning to watch the sunrise over the water."

James nodded, lost in the past. "And we'd spend the afternoons swimming and fishing. Do you remember the time you caught that huge bass and refused to let me help you reel it in?"

Sarah laughed, the sound filled with warmth and nostalgia. "Yes! I was so stubborn. But I did it, didn't I?"

"You did," James said, his voice soft. "And those nights by the campfire, just the two of us under the stars... I've never felt so at peace."

Sarah squeezed his hand. "Me neither. Those were simple times, happy times."

James sighed, a mix of contentment and longing in his expression. "I used to think about those nights whenever I was feeling down. They always brought me a sense of calm."

Sarah looked at him, her eyes reflecting the same emotions. "I did too. Especially during those tough days when I was traveling alone for work. I'd think back to us, and it made things a bit easier."

James felt a lump in his throat, the reality of their shared past hitting him hard. "We had something special, Sarah. Maybe it was just bad timing."

Sarah's eyes glistened with unshed tears. "Maybe. But I believe everything happens for a reason. Look at us now, meeting again after all these years."

They talked for hours, their conversation flowing easily, the years apart melting away. They laughed about old times, shared their dreams and regrets. The café grew quiet as the night wore on, but they barely noticed.

As the evening turned into night, James felt a sense of contentment he hadn't felt in years. Being with Sarah felt right, like a missing piece of his life had fallen into place. He looked at her, his heart full.

"I'm really glad we met again, Sarah," he said softly. "I've missed this. I've missed you."

Sarah's eyes glistened with unshed tears. "Me too, James. Me too."

They lingered a bit longer, savoring the moment. When it was finally time to part, they exchanged numbers, promising to stay in touch. As James watched Sarah walk away, a sense of hope bloomed within him. He knew their story was far from over.

Chapter 3: Crossing the Line

The moon hung low in the sky, casting a soft, silvery glow over the quiet streets. James and Sarah walked side by side, the cool evening air wrapping around them like a comforting blanket. They had left the café hours ago, their conversation having flowed seamlessly from one topic to another. Now, they found themselves at a small, secluded park, the sounds of the city a distant hum.

James glanced at Sarah, her auburn hair shimmering under the moonlight. She wore a thoughtful expression, her black dress accentuating her graceful figure. His heart pounded in his chest, a mix of excitement and anxiety swirling within him.

"This place is beautiful," Sarah said, her voice a soft whisper.

"It is," James agreed, his eyes never leaving her face. "I'm really glad we came here."

They found a bench near the edge of the park, the soft rustle of leaves providing a gentle backdrop to their conversation. Sarah sat down first, smoothing her dress, while James took a seat beside her, the space between them charged with unspoken tension.

"Do you ever think about the past?" Sarah asked, her gaze fixed on the stars above.

"All the time," James replied, his voice low and earnest. "Especially about us. We had something special, Sarah."

Sarah turned to look at him, her eyes reflecting the same mix of emotions he felt. "I think about it too. Sometimes I wonder what might have been if things had been different."

James reached out, taking her hand in his. The touch sent a jolt through him, a reminder of the connection they once shared. "I've missed you so much. More than I can put into words."

Sarah squeezed his hand, her eyes filling with tears. "I've missed you too, James. It's like a part of me has always been with you."

They sat in silence for a moment, the weight of their words hanging in the air. The world around them seemed to fade away, leaving only the two of them in a cocoon of shared memories and unspoken desires.

James leaned closer, his heart racing. "Sarah, I... I still have feelings for you. I know it's complicated, but I can't help how I feel."

Sarah's breath caught in her throat, her eyes searching his. "James, I feel the same way. But what about your family? Your wife?"

James sighed, the reality of his situation crashing down on him. "I know it's not fair. But my marriage... it's been over for a long time. We're just going through the motions for Max's sake."

Sarah's tears spilled over, her voice trembling. "I don't want to be the cause of more pain for you, James. But being with you feels right. It feels like coming home."

James cupped her face in his hands, his touch gentle and reassuring. "You are home, Sarah. With you, I feel alive again."

Their faces inched closer, the tension between them building to a crescendo. James could feel her breath on his lips, the anticipation electric. The world around them disappeared as they closed the distance, their lips finally meeting in a kiss that felt like the culmination of years of longing.

The kiss deepened, their emotions pouring out in a passionate embrace. James pulled her closer, his hands tangling in her hair. Sarah responded with equal fervor, her arms wrapping around his neck. The kiss was a promise, a declaration of the love they still held for each other.

When they finally pulled apart, they were both breathless, their foreheads resting against each other. James looked into Sarah's eyes, his heart full. "I love you, Sarah. I always have."

"I love you too, James," Sarah whispered, her voice filled with emotion. "I never stopped."

They sat there, holding each other, the weight of their love and the reality of their situation pressing down on them. But in that moment, they were together, and that was all that mattered. The line between past and present had been crossed, and there was no turning back.

Chapter 4: Guilty Pleasures

James stepped out of the cab, the cool night air brushing against his face. The exhilaration from the evening with Sarah still coursed through him, mingling with a heavy sense of guilt. He approached the front door of his suburban home, the familiar sight now tinged with a newfound uncertainty. He paused, taking a deep breath before turning the key in the lock.

The house was quiet, dimly lit by the soft glow of a table lamp in the living room. James slipped off his shoes and hung his coat, his mind replaying the events of the evening. He could still feel Sarah's touch, her kiss lingering on his lips. The warmth of her presence contrasted sharply with the coldness he felt at home.

Emily sat on the couch, dressed in a comfortable, worn-out robe, her face illuminated by the flickering light of the television. She glanced up as James entered, her eyes narrowing slightly.

"You're late," she said, her voice devoid of emotion.

James forced a smile, his heart pounding. "Yeah, the conference ran longer than expected. Sorry about that."

Emily's gaze lingered on him, a mixture of suspicion and indifference in her eyes. "Did you eat?"

James nodded, walking over to sit on the armchair opposite her. "Yeah, grabbed something on the way back."

The silence between them was heavy, the tension palpable. James could feel Emily's eyes on him, probing, searching for something. He shifted uncomfortably, his mind racing with thoughts of Sarah and the guilt gnawing at him.

"You seem... different," Emily said finally, her tone cold. "Is there something you want to tell me?"

James' heart skipped a beat. He forced himself to meet her gaze, the weight of his actions pressing down on him. "No, just tired. It's been a long day."

Emily's eyes flashed with anger. "Bullshit, James. I can see it all over your face. Something's going on. You're hiding something from me."

James felt a surge of defensiveness. "Emily, you're imagining things. I'm just tired, okay?"

Emily stood up, her robe swishing angrily around her. "Imagining things? You think I'm stupid? I know you, James. I know when something's off. What is it? Another woman?"

James' stomach dropped, and he struggled to keep his composure. "That's ridiculous. Why would you even say that?"

Emily took a step closer, her eyes blazing. "Because you're never here! You're always off on some trip or staying late at work. I'm not blind, James. I see how distant you've become. What the hell is going on?"

James clenched his fists, trying to control his temper. "Emily, I'm doing my best to provide for this family. You know how demanding my job is."

Emily laughed bitterly. "Provide? You think throwing money at us is enough? We need you here, James. Max needs his father. I need my husband."

James felt a pang of guilt, the truth of her words cutting deep. "I'm trying, Emily. It's not that simple."

"Not that simple?" Emily's voice rose, trembling with rage. "You made it simple when you decided to put your job above everything else. We're falling apart, and you don't even see it. Or maybe you just don't care."

James stood up, facing her. "That's not fair. I'm here now, aren't I?"

Emily's eyes filled with tears, her voice breaking. "Physically, maybe. But emotionally? You've been gone for years. I don't even know who you are anymore."

The words hit James like a punch to the gut. He took a deep breath, trying to steady himself. "I'm sorry, Emily. I know I haven't been the best husband. But accusing me of cheating? That's too much."

Emily wiped her eyes angrily. "Is it? Because right now, I don't even know if I trust you."

James felt the room spinning, his emotions in turmoil. "I've never given you a reason to doubt me."

Emily shook her head. "Maybe not before. But things have changed, James. I feel like I'm living with a stranger."

The silence between them was heavy, the tension almost unbearable. James could see the hurt in Emily's eyes, and it tore at him. He reached out, placing a tentative hand on her shoulder. "Emily, I'm sorry. I don't know how we got here, but I want to fix this."

Emily looked at him, her expression a mixture of anger and sadness. "Do you? Because it doesn't feel like it. It feels like you're just going through the motions."

James dropped his hand, feeling helpless. "What do you want me to do?"

Emily sighed, her voice weary. "I don't know, James. I just know something has to change. I can't keep living like this."

James watched her walk away, his heart heavy with guilt and regret. The house felt colder, emptier than ever. He knew he had to make a choice, but the path ahead seemed anything but clear. The thrill of being with Sarah, the guilt of betraying Emily, the responsibility to his family—all these emotions swirled within him, leaving him feeling more conflicted than ever.

He finished his water and turned off the kitchen light, the house now enveloped in darkness. As he climbed the stairs, each step felt heavier than the last. He paused outside the bedroom door, listening to the quiet sounds of Emily settling into bed. Steeling himself, he entered the room, slipping into the familiar but now strained space beside his wife.

Emily lay on her side, her back to him. The distance between them felt insurmountable, a chasm that had grown over years of neglect and unspoken resentments. James lay there, staring at the ceiling, the silence pressing down on him.

He reached out, placing a tentative hand on Emily's shoulder. She stiffened but didn't pull away. "Goodnight, Emily," he whispered, his voice heavy with the weight of his actions.

She replied nothing. feeling distant.

James closed his eyes, the guilt and exhilaration from the evening mixing into a confusing haze. As he lay there, the memory of Sarah's touch and the cold reality of his marriage played out in his mind, leaving him restless and unsure of what the future would hold.

Chapter 5: Old Flames, New Fires

James parked his car a few blocks away from Sarah's house, the quiet suburban street bathed in the soft glow of streetlights. His heart pounded with anticipation and guilt, a complex mix of emotions he couldn't fully disentangle. He walked briskly, hands in his pockets, the cool night air doing little to calm his racing thoughts.

Sarah's house was a charming, two-story home with ivy climbing the brick walls and a well-tended garden. He approached the front door, taking a deep breath before ringing the bell. Moments later, the door swung open, and there she stood, a vision in a simple yet elegant dress that hugged her curves. Her auburn hair framed her face, her eyes bright with excitement.

"James," she breathed, her voice filled with warmth. "I'm so glad you're here."

James stepped inside, closing the door behind him. The scent of lavender and vanilla enveloped him, a stark contrast to the cold, sterile atmosphere of his own home. He pulled Sarah into his arms, their bodies fitting together as if no time had passed since their last embrace.

"I've missed you," he whispered into her hair, his voice heavy with emotion.

Sarah looked up at him, her eyes reflecting the same longing he felt. "I've missed you too. Come, let's go to the living room."

They moved to the living room, a cozy space filled with soft lighting and plush furniture. A fire crackled in the fireplace, casting a warm glow across the room. Sarah led him to the couch, where they sat close, their hands entwined.

"How have you been?" James asked, his thumb caressing the back of her hand.

"Better now that you're here," Sarah replied, her smile radiant. "Work has been hectic, but thinking about you... it makes everything better."

James leaned in, his lips brushing against hers in a tender kiss. "Being with you feels right, Sarah. I don't know how to explain it."

Sarah's eyes darkened with intensity. "You don't have to explain. I feel the same way. It's like we've found something we lost a long time ago."

They kissed again, this time more passionately. The world outside faded away, leaving only the two of them in their bubble of rediscovered love. James' hands roamed her back, pulling her closer as their kiss deepened. Sarah responded with equal fervor, her fingers tangling in his hair.

"I want you, James," she whispered against his lips, her voice husky with desire. "I need you."

James' heart raced, the urgency of their need for each other overwhelming him. "I need you too, Sarah. More than you know."

They moved to the bedroom, a haven of warmth and intimacy. The room was dimly lit, the soft glow of candles casting flickering shadows on the walls. Sarah's bed, adorned with plush pillows and a thick, inviting comforter, beckoned to them. They undressed slowly, savoring the anticipation and the feel of each other's skin.

As they lay together, their bodies entwined, the intensity of their connection reignited the passion they once shared. Every touch, every kiss was a testament to their deep, unspoken bond. They moved together in perfect harmony, their lovemaking an exquisite blend of tenderness and desire.

Afterward, they lay in each other's arms, the sound of their breathing the only noise in the room. James traced patterns on Sarah's bare back, his mind a whirlwind of thoughts and emotions.

"James," Sarah murmured, breaking the silence. "What are we going to do?"

James sighed, the reality of their situation crashing down on him. "I don't know. I just know I can't stay away from you."

Sarah propped herself up on one elbow, looking down at him. "I don't want to come between you and your family. But I can't let you go, either."

James reached up, cupping her face in his hand. "We'll figure it out. I don't have all the answers, but I know I need you in my life."

Tears glistened in Sarah's eyes. "I need you too, James. More than anything."

They lay together in silence, the weight of their love and the complications it brought pressing down on them. The fire in the living room crackled softly, the warmth a stark contrast to the cold uncertainty they faced.

James spent the night at Sarah's, their bodies intertwined under the covers. In the quiet moments before sleep claimed him, he felt a sense of peace he hadn't felt in years. Being with Sarah was like coming home, a place where he could be himself without fear or pretension.

The next morning, sunlight streamed through the curtains, casting a golden glow over the room. James woke to find Sarah watching him, her expression soft and filled with love.

"Morning," she said, her voice a gentle caress.

"Morning," James replied, leaning in to kiss her. "Last night was... incredible."

Sarah smiled, a hint of sadness in her eyes. "It was. But what now?"

James took a deep breath, the reality of their situation settling over him once more. "I don't know. But we'll figure it out together."

They shared a quiet breakfast, savoring the stolen moments of normalcy. James knew he had to leave soon, return to the life that awaited him. But for now, he focused on the here and now, the feel of Sarah's hand in his, the taste of her lips on his.

As he walked back to his car, he felt a renewed sense of purpose. The path ahead was fraught with challenges, but he knew one thing for certain: he couldn't turn his back on the love he had found again.

Chapter 6: Strained Ties

The morning sun filtered through the kitchen window, casting a soft glow over the breakfast table. James sat across from Max, sipping his coffee and reading the newspaper. Max, dressed in his school uniform, pushed his cereal around his bowl, his expression distant.

Emily entered the kitchen, her movements tense and deliberate. She wore a simple blouse and jeans, her face set in a hard line. James glanced up, offering a tentative smile.

"Morning," he said, trying to keep his tone light.

Emily barely acknowledged him, her eyes cold. "Morning."

The tension in the room was palpable. James could feel Emily's resentment growing stronger each day. He had been spending more time with Sarah, and his absences were becoming increasingly noticeable.

Max looked between his parents, sensing the strain. "Dad, are you going to be home tonight?"

James hesitated, glancing at Emily. "I'm not sure, buddy. I might have to work late."

Emily's eyes narrowed, her lips pressing into a thin line. "Of course you do. Always working late."

James sighed, setting down his coffee cup. "Emily, I have responsibilities. You know that."

Emily crossed her arms, her voice dripping with sarcasm. "Responsibilities. Right. Because your job is so much more important than your family."

Max shifted uncomfortably in his seat, looking down at his cereal. James reached out, placing a hand on his son's shoulder. "Max, finish your breakfast. You'll be late for school."

Max nodded, quickly eating his cereal. Emily watched them, her expression a mix of anger and hurt. When Max left the room, she turned her full attention to James.

"Do you think I'm stupid, James?" she demanded, her voice low and fierce.

James blinked, taken aback. "What are you talking about?"

Emily's eyes flashed with fury. "I know you're hiding something. You're always gone, and when you are here, you're distant. What is it, James? Another woman?"

James' heart skipped a beat, guilt flooding his veins. "Emily, that's not fair. I'm working hard to provide for this family."

Emily laughed bitterly. "Provide? Is that what you call it? You're never here. Max barely sees you, and I... I feel like I don't even know you anymore."

James ran a hand through his hair, frustration boiling over. "I'm trying, Emily. I'm doing my best."

Emily's voice broke, tears welling up in her eyes. "Your best? Your best isn't good enough. We're falling apart, and you don't even see it."

James felt a pang of guilt, the truth of her words hitting him hard. He reached out, trying to take her hand, but she pulled away. "Emily, please. Let's talk about this."

Emily shook her head, her tears spilling over. "Talk? What's there to talk about? You've already made your choice."

James stood up, his own emotions threatening to overwhelm him. "That's not true. I love you and Max. I don't want to lose this family."

Emily looked at him, her expression one of deep sadness and resignation. "Then prove it, James. Be here. Be present. Because right now, I feel like I'm losing you."

James opened his mouth to respond, but the words wouldn't come. He watched as Emily turned and left the room, her shoulders shaking with silent sobs. He sank back into his chair, his head in his hands. The weight of his actions pressed down on him, the guilt and regret almost too much to bear.

That evening, James sat in his car outside Sarah's house, his mind racing. He had to make a decision, one that would impact everyone he cared about. He couldn't keep living a double life, torn between two worlds. He took a deep breath, trying to steady his nerves. He had to face the truth, no matter how painful.

When he returned home, the house was dark and quiet. He found Emily in the living room, sitting on the couch with a blanket wrapped around her. She looked up as he entered, her eyes red and swollen from crying.

"Emily," he began, his voice trembling. "We need to talk."

Emily nodded, her expression wary. "Yes, we do."

James sat down beside her, the silence between them heavy with unspoken words. He reached out, taking her hand in his. "I've been lying to you. There is someone else."

Emily's breath caught, her eyes widening with shock and hurt. "How could you, James? After everything we've been through?"

James felt his own tears start to fall. "I'm so sorry, Emily. I never wanted to hurt you. I just... I got lost. But I love you, and I want to make this right."

Emily pulled her hand away, her voice trembling. "I don't know if we can make this right, James. I don't know if I can ever trust you again."

James nodded, his heart breaking. "I understand. But I'm willing to do whatever it takes to fix this. For you, for Max, for our family."

Emily looked at him for a long moment, her eyes searching his. Finally, she spoke, her voice soft but firm. "We'll see, James. But things have to change. Starting now."

James nodded, the weight of her words sinking in. He knew it wouldn't be easy, but he was determined to do whatever it took to rebuild the trust he had shattered. As they sat together in the dimly lit living room, the path ahead seemed uncertain, but for the first time in a long while, James felt a glimmer of hope.

Chapter 7: The Balancing Act

James sat at his desk in the study, the dim glow of the lamp casting long shadows across the room. His laptop screen displayed a spreadsheet, but his mind was elsewhere. The weight of his dual life pressed heavily on his shoulders, the strain of balancing his family and his affair with Sarah growing more unbearable each day.

He glanced at the clock. It was nearly midnight, and he knew he should go to bed, but his thoughts were too tangled to find rest. The door creaked open, and Emily stepped in, wearing a worn-out robe and a weary expression.

"James, are you coming to bed?" she asked, her voice soft but tinged with sadness.

James looked up, forcing a smile. "In a bit. I just need to finish this."

Emily nodded, her eyes reflecting the distance between them. "Don't stay up too late."

She left the room, and James leaned back in his chair, rubbing his temples. The guilt gnawed at him, the pull between his duty to his family and his desire for Sarah tearing him apart.

The next morning, the household buzzed with activity. Max was getting ready for school, his backpack slung over one shoulder. Emily stood by the kitchen counter, preparing breakfast. James joined them, trying to maintain a semblance of normalcy.

"Morning, Max," James said, ruffling his son's hair. "Ready for school?"

Max nodded, a slight smile on his face. "Yeah, Dad. Got a big test today."

Emily placed a plate of pancakes on the table, her expression neutral. "Good luck with your test, Max."

James watched them, the mundane routine feeling like a fragile facade. He poured himself a cup of coffee, trying to shake off the lingering unease.

Later that day, James found himself at Sarah's house, the sanctuary where he could momentarily forget his troubles. Sarah greeted him with a warm embrace, her auburn hair brushing against his cheek.

"James, I've missed you," she whispered, her voice a balm to his frayed nerves.

"I've missed you too," James replied, holding her close. "It's been so hard, Sarah. I don't know how much longer I can keep this up."

They moved to the living room, where they sat on the couch, their hands intertwined. Sarah looked at him, concern etched in her features. "James, you need to make a decision. This... balancing act is tearing you apart."

James sighed, his heart heavy. "I know. But I can't just walk away from my family. Max needs me. Emily... she deserves better than this."

Sarah squeezed his hand, her eyes filled with understanding. "And what about us? What about what we have?"

James leaned in, pressing a kiss to her forehead. "I love you, Sarah. I do. But I'm trapped between two worlds, and I don't know how to make it right."

That evening, James returned home, the tension in the house palpable. Emily was in the living room, reading a book. Max was in his room, the faint sound of music drifting down the hall. James took a deep breath, steeling himself for the conversation he knew he needed to have.

"Emily," he said, sitting down beside her. "We need to talk."

Emily looked up from her book, her expression wary. "What is it, James?"

James took her hand, his voice trembling. "I've been struggling. Trying to be everything to everyone, and I'm failing. I know I've been distant, and I'm sorry."

Emily's eyes softened, but the hurt was still there. "I just want us to be a family again, James. I want you to be present, for me and for Max."

James nodded, tears pricking at the corners of his eyes. "I want that too. I don't know how to fix this, but I'm willing to try."

Emily squeezed his hand, a glimmer of hope in her eyes. "Then let's try. For us, and for Max."

James spent the next few days trying to find a balance, dividing his time between his family and his secret meetings with Sarah. The strain was evident, the cracks in his carefully constructed facade growing wider. He knew he couldn't continue like this, but the thought of losing Sarah or his family was unbearable.

One afternoon, as he sat in a café with Sarah, he voiced his fears. "Sarah, I'm at a breaking point. I can't keep living like this."

Sarah reached across the table, taking his hand. "James, you have to make a choice. I can't keep being the other woman. You need to decide where your heart truly lies."

James looked at her, the love he felt for her warring with his sense of duty. "I don't want to lose you, Sarah. But I can't abandon my family."

Sarah's eyes filled with tears. "I don't want to lose you either, James. But you can't have it both ways."

That night, James lay in bed, staring at the ceiling, the weight of his dilemma pressing down on him. Emily lay beside him, her breathing steady and calm. He knew he had to make a decision, one that would change all their lives forever.

In the quiet of the night, James resolved to face the truth. He couldn't keep living a lie, torn between duty and desire. The path ahead was uncertain, but he knew he had to find a way to reconcile his heart and his responsibilities, for his sake and for the sake of those he loved.

Chapter 8: Whispered Secrets

James parked his car in a secluded spot a few blocks from Sarah's house, his heart racing with anticipation. The late afternoon sun cast long shadows over the quiet neighborhood, a stark contrast to the turmoil within him. He checked his watch, then walked briskly to Sarah's front door, his mind a whirlwind of excitement and guilt.

Sarah opened the door before he could knock, a smile spreading across her face. She wore a simple, elegant dress that accentuated her curves, her auburn hair falling in loose waves around her shoulders.

"James," she said softly, pulling him into a warm embrace. "I'm so glad you're here."

James held her close, the scent of lavender and vanilla enveloping him. "I couldn't stay away," he whispered, kissing her gently. "I've missed you."

They moved inside, the house a sanctuary from the outside world. The living room was dimly lit, the soft glow of candles creating a warm, intimate atmosphere. They settled on the couch, their hands entwined, the weight of their secret heavy but thrilling.

"How was your day?" Sarah asked, her eyes reflecting the depth of her emotions.

James sighed, a mix of exhaustion and excitement. "It was long. All I could think about was being here with you."

Sarah smiled, leaning in to kiss him. "I've been thinking about you too. I can't get you out of my mind, James."

Their kisses grew more passionate, their bodies pressing closer. The intensity of their desire filled the room, the connection between them undeniable. James traced his fingers along Sarah's jawline, his touch sending shivers down her spine.

"Sarah," he murmured, his voice husky with emotion. "I want you. I need you."

Sarah's eyes darkened with desire. "I need you too, James. More than anything."

They moved to the bedroom, the anticipation palpable. The room was a haven of warmth and intimacy, the bed inviting with its plush pillows and soft comforter. They undressed slowly, savoring the moment, their eyes never leaving each other.

As they lay together, exploring each other's bodies, the intensity of their connection deepened. Every touch, every kiss was filled with unspoken words, their deepest desires laid bare. The outside world ceased to exist, leaving only the two of them in their cocoon of passion and love.

Afterward, they lay entwined under the covers, the soft glow of the candles casting flickering shadows on the walls. James traced lazy patterns on Sarah's back, his mind a mix of contentment and conflict.

"James," Sarah said softly, breaking the comfortable silence. "What are we going to do?"

James sighed, pulling her closer. "I don't know, Sarah. I hate hiding, but I can't lose you."

Sarah propped herself up on one elbow, looking into his eyes. "I can't lose you either. But this... it's so complicated."

James nodded, his heart heavy. "I know. But being with you feels right. It's the only time I feel truly alive."

Sarah's eyes filled with tears. "I feel the same way. But I don't want to hurt anyone."

James kissed her gently, his lips lingering on hers. "We'll figure it out, Sarah. I promise."

They spent the evening in each other's arms, their whispered secrets filling the room. The intensity of their affair grew with each passing day, the line between duty and desire blurring more and more. They met in secret, their passion for each other consuming them, the thrill of their forbidden love both exhilarating and terrifying.

James found himself living for these moments with Sarah, the rest of his life fading into the background. The secrecy added a layer of intensity, each stolen moment a precious treasure. They explored their deepest desires, their connection deepening in ways neither had anticipated.

But with each meeting, the reality of their situation loomed larger. James knew they couldn't continue like this forever, but the thought of ending their affair was unbearable. The balancing act became more precarious, the stakes higher with every encounter.

As they lay together one evening, their bodies entwined, James voiced the fear that had been growing inside him. "What if we get caught, Sarah? What if this all comes crashing down?"

Sarah looked at him, her eyes filled with a mixture of love and fear. "I don't know, James. But I can't imagine my life without you."

James kissed her, his heart aching with the weight of their love and the complexity of their situation. "We'll find a way, Sarah. We have to."

Their whispered secrets continued to bind them together, the intensity of their affair a blazing fire that neither could extinguish. They clung to each other, their love a beacon in the darkness, even as the world around them threatened to unravel.

Chapter 9: Cracks in the Façade

James sat at the dining table, staring blankly at the cold remnants of dinner. Emily had already cleared her plate, and Max was in his room, likely doing homework or playing video games. The silence in the house was deafening, a stark contrast to the usual buzz of family life. Emily walked back into the room, her face set in a hard, determined expression. She wore a simple blouse and jeans, her hair pulled back into a tight ponytail.

"James, we need to talk," she said, her voice firm.

James looked up, a knot forming in his stomach. "Sure, Emily. What's on your mind?"

Emily sat down across from him, her eyes searching his face. "What's going on with you? You've been so distant lately. You're never home, and when you are, it's like you're a million miles away."

James took a deep breath, trying to steady his nerves. "I've been busy with work. You know how demanding it can be."

Emily's eyes narrowed, a flash of anger crossing her features. "Don't give me that. This is more than just work. You barely spend time with Max, and you barely talk to me. Something's changed, and I want to know what it is."

James felt a surge of guilt and defensiveness. "I'm doing my best, Emily. I'm trying to balance everything."

Emily's voice rose, trembling with emotion. "Your best? James, you're not even here! Max needs his father, and I need my husband. What are you hiding from us?"

James looked away, unable to meet her gaze. "It's not that simple."

Emily leaned forward, her eyes blazing. "Then make it simple, James. Tell me the truth. Are you seeing someone else?"

James' heart pounded, the weight of his secret threatening to crush him. He opened his mouth to speak, but the words wouldn't come.

Emily's eyes filled with tears, her voice breaking. "I knew it. I could feel it. How could you do this to us? To me? To Max?"

James reached out, desperate to comfort her. "Emily, I'm so sorry. I never wanted to hurt you."

Emily pulled away, her tears spilling over. "Sorry? You're sorry? That's all you have to say? Do you even realize what you've done to this family?"

James felt his own tears start to fall. "I know I've messed up. I know I've hurt you. But I love you and Max. I don't want to lose our family."

Emily stood up, her voice shaking with anger and pain. "Love? You call this love? James, you've been lying to us, living a double life. How can I ever trust you again?"

James looked down at his hands, the weight of her words pressing down on him. "I don't know. But I'm willing to do whatever it takes to make this right."

Emily shook her head, her expression one of deep sadness and betrayal. "I don't know if that's possible. The damage is done, James. And I don't know if we can ever fix it."

James felt a wave of despair wash over him. "Please, Emily. Give me a chance. Let me prove that I can change."

Emily took a deep breath, her eyes filled with a mixture of anger and heartbreak. "We'll see, James. But things have to change. Starting now."

As she walked away, James felt the full weight of his actions crashing down on him. The cracks in the facade of their perfect family life were widening, threatening to shatter everything they had built. He knew he had a long, difficult road ahead if he wanted to repair the damage he had caused.

Later that night, James found himself sitting on the edge of Max's bed. Max looked up from his book, his expression filled with concern.

"Dad, is everything okay? I heard you and Mom fighting."

James sighed, reaching out to ruffle Max's hair. "It's complicated, buddy. But your mom and I are going to try and work things out."

Max's eyes searched his father's face, looking for reassurance. "I just want us to be a family again. Like we used to be."

James felt a lump form in his throat. "Me too, Max. Me too."

As he left Max's room, James couldn't shake the feeling that their family was hanging by a thread. The tension in the house was palpable, every interaction fraught with the unspoken pain and betrayal that lay just beneath the surface.

In the days that followed, James tried to bridge the gap between him and Emily, but the distance seemed insurmountable. He spent more time at home, trying to be present for Max, but the strain of his secret life with Sarah weighed heavily on him.

One evening, as they sat in the living room, Emily turned to him, her eyes filled with a mix of sadness and resolve. "James, I can't keep living like this. We need to make a decision about our future."

James nodded, his heart heavy with the knowledge that their lives were at a crossroads. "I know, Emily. And I'm ready to do whatever it takes to make things right."

As they talked late into the night, the reality of their situation became painfully clear. The road to healing and rebuilding trust would be long and arduous, and there were no guarantees. But for the sake of their family, James knew he had to try. The cracks in the facade of their perfect life had been exposed, and now it was up to him to find a way to mend the broken pieces.

Chapter 10: Escape

James drove down the winding road, the trees on either side forming a canopy that filtered the late afternoon sunlight. The air was crisp, a welcome change from the stifling tension at home. Sarah sat beside him, her hair blowing softly in the breeze from the open window. She wore a light summer dress that fluttered with the movement of the car, her eyes sparkling with excitement.

"Where are we going?" Sarah asked, her voice filled with curiosity and delight.

James smiled, glancing over at her. "It's a surprise. Just a little escape for us."

Sarah reached over, placing her hand on his. "I love surprises."

They drove for another hour, the city gradually giving way to rolling hills and open fields. The tension in James's shoulders began to ease, the weight of his problems momentarily forgotten. He felt a sense of freedom he hadn't experienced in a long time, the thrill of spontaneity filling his heart.

They arrived at a secluded cabin nestled by a tranquil lake, the water reflecting the golden hues of the setting sun. James parked the car and got out, walking around to open Sarah's door. She stepped out, looking around in awe.

"James, this is beautiful," she whispered, her eyes wide with wonder.

"I thought you'd like it," he replied, wrapping an arm around her waist. "Come on, let's go inside."

The cabin was cozy and inviting, with rustic wooden furniture and a large stone fireplace. James had planned ahead, stocking the kitchen with everything they might need for their stay. Sarah wandered around, admiring the simplicity and charm of the place.

"This is perfect," she said, turning to face him. "Thank you for bringing me here."

James pulled her close, kissing her softly. "You deserve it, Sarah. We both needed this."

They spent the evening exploring the area around the cabin, walking hand in hand along the lakeshore. The air was filled with the sounds of nature, the gentle rustling of leaves and the distant call of birds. As the sun dipped below the horizon, they returned to the cabin, a sense of peace settling over them.

Inside, James lit a fire in the fireplace, the warm glow filling the room. Sarah prepared a simple dinner, the aroma of cooked food mingling with the scent of pine from the surrounding woods. They ate by the fire, their conversation flowing easily, the worries of the outside world slipping away.

"Tell me more about your dreams, James," Sarah said, her eyes reflecting the flickering flames.

James leaned back, a thoughtful expression on his face. "I've always dreamed of a life where I could just be myself. No pretenses, no masks. Just... real."

Sarah reached across the table, taking his hand. "You can have that, James. We can have that. Together."

James squeezed her hand, his heart swelling with love and hope. "I want that more than anything, Sarah. Being with you feels like coming home."

Later, they sat on the porch, wrapped in a blanket, watching the stars appear in the night sky. The air was cool and refreshing, the silence filled with a sense of possibility.

"James," Sarah said softly, her head resting on his shoulder. "What happens when we go back? To reality?"

James sighed, his breath visible in the cool air. "I don't know, Sarah. But I do know that I want to face it with you. We'll figure it out, one step at a time."

Sarah looked up at him, her eyes filled with trust and determination. "I believe in us, James. I believe we can make it work."

He kissed her forehead, his heart full. "I believe in us too."

They stayed like that for a long time, finding comfort in each other's presence. The cabin and the lake became their sanctuary, a place where they could be their true selves, free from judgment and fear.

The next morning, they woke to the sound of birds singing, the sunlight streaming through the windows. They spent the day exploring the woods, laughing and talking, their bond growing stronger with each shared moment. James felt a renewed sense of purpose, the love he shared with Sarah giving him the strength to face whatever lay ahead.

As they packed up to leave, Sarah turned to James, her eyes shining. "This has been the best escape ever. Thank you."

James smiled, pulling her into a tight embrace. "Thank you, Sarah. For everything."

They drove back to the city, the memory of their time at the cabin a precious treasure they would carry with them. James knew the road ahead would be challenging, but he felt ready to face it, knowing that he and Sarah were stronger together.

Chapter 11: The Turning Point

James sat at the kitchen table, the morning light streaming through the windows. He sipped his coffee, trying to focus on the newspaper in front of him. Emily moved around the kitchen, her movements tense and hurried. She wore a navy blouse and jeans, her face set in a permanent frown. Max shuffled into the room, his backpack slung over one shoulder, his eyes downcast.

"Morning, Max," James said, attempting a cheerful tone.

"Morning," Max mumbled, barely glancing at his father.

Emily placed a plate of toast on the table, her eyes briefly meeting James's before she turned away. "Max, hurry up and eat. You'll be late for school."

Max sat down, picking at his toast without enthusiasm. James watched him, a knot forming in his stomach. "How's school going, buddy? Everything okay?"

Max shrugged, his shoulders slumping. "It's fine, I guess."

James exchanged a worried glance with Emily. She sighed, leaning against the counter. "Max, is there something you want to talk about? You've been so quiet lately."

Max shook his head, his eyes fixed on his plate. "No, Mom. I'm fine."

James reached out, placing a hand on Max's arm. "You know you can talk to us about anything, right? We're here for you."

Max pulled away, his voice barely above a whisper. "I said I'm fine."

The tension in the room was palpable, the silence stretching on uncomfortably. James and Emily exchanged another worried glance, both feeling helpless.

That afternoon, James received a call from Max's school. The principal's voice was serious, her words echoing in his mind. "Mr. Carter, we've noticed a significant drop in Max's performance lately. He's been withdrawn, and his grades are slipping. We think it might be best if you and your wife came in for a meeting."

James thanked her and hung up, his heart sinking. He knew the strain between him and Emily was affecting Max more than they had realized. He called Emily, telling her about the meeting. Her voice was strained but resigned. "We'll be there, James. We need to figure out how to help him."

That evening, they sat in the living room, the atmosphere heavy with unspoken worries. Max was in his room, the door closed. James looked at Emily, his heart aching with guilt. "We need to do something, Emily. This is affecting Max more than we thought."

Emily nodded, her eyes filled with sadness. "I know. We have to find a way to make things better for him. He deserves more than this."

The next day, they sat in the principal's office, the tension between them evident. The principal, Mrs. Harris, looked at them with concern. "Max is a bright student, but he's been struggling lately. We believe the issues at home might be affecting him."

James felt a pang of guilt, his eyes meeting Emily's. "We know things have been tough at home. We're trying to work through it."

Mrs. Harris nodded. "It's important that Max feels supported and heard. Maybe counseling could help, both for him and for your family."

James and Emily agreed, their resolve to help Max stronger than ever. They knew they had to put aside their differences, at least for now, to focus on their son's well-being.

At home, James knocked on Max's door, waiting for a response. When none came, he gently pushed the door open. Max was sitting at his desk, his head in his hands.

"Max, can we talk?" James asked softly.

Max looked up, his eyes red. "What is it, Dad?"

James walked over, sitting down beside him. "Mom and I are worried about you. We know things have been tough lately, and we're sorry if we've made you feel like you're caught in the middle."

Max's voice trembled. "I just want things to go back to the way they were. I hate it when you and Mom fight."

James felt his heart break, tears welling up in his eyes. "I know, buddy. We're trying to fix things. We want to make it better for you."

Max looked at him, his eyes filled with a mix of hope and fear. "Promise?"

James nodded, pulling Max into a hug. "I promise, Max. We'll get through this together."

The following weeks were challenging, but James and Emily worked hard to create a more stable environment for Max. They attended counseling sessions, both individually and as a family. Slowly, they began to rebuild the trust that had been shattered.

James made a conscious effort to be more present, spending quality time with Max. They went to his soccer games, worked on homework together, and even started a new hobby: building model airplanes.

One evening, as they sat at the dining table working on a particularly challenging model, Max looked up at James, a small smile on his face. "Thanks for being here, Dad."

James felt a surge of emotion, his heart swelling with love and pride. "Always, Max. I'm always here for you."

Emily walked into the room, her expression softer than it had been in weeks. She joined them at the table, her presence a silent promise that they were all in this together.

The cracks in their family were still there, but they were beginning to heal. With each passing day, they grew stronger, finding comfort in the love they shared. The turning point had been difficult, but it had brought them closer, reminding them of what truly mattered.

Chapter 12: The Confession

James sat on the edge of the bed in Sarah's apartment, the dim light from the bedside lamp casting a soft glow over the room. Sarah stood by the window, looking out at the city lights. She wore a simple, flowing dress, her auburn hair cascading down her back. The atmosphere was heavy with unspoken words, the tension palpable.

"James," Sarah began, her voice trembling slightly. "We need to talk about us."

James felt a knot form in his stomach. He knew this conversation was coming, but he wasn't prepared. "I know, Sarah. I've been thinking about it a lot."

Sarah turned to face him, her eyes filled with a mixture of hope and fear. "What are we doing, James? This... affair, it can't go on like this. We need to decide what we want for our future."

James looked down at his hands, his heart heavy. "I'm so conflicted, Sarah. I love you, but my family... Max, Emily... they need me too."

Sarah walked over and sat beside him, taking his hands in hers. "I understand that, James. But what about us? What do we mean to each other?"

James looked into her eyes, his heart aching with the weight of his emotions. "You mean everything to me, Sarah. Being with you feels right, like I've found a part of myself I didn't know was missing."

Sarah's eyes filled with tears. "I feel the same way, James. But I can't keep living in the shadows, hiding our love. It's tearing me apart."

James felt a surge of guilt and sorrow. "I don't want to hurt you, Sarah. I don't want to lose you. But I don't know how to make this work."

Sarah's grip on his hands tightened. "Promise me, James. Promise me that we'll find a way to be together. I can't go on like this, not knowing where we stand."

James took a deep breath, his mind racing. He knew he had to make a commitment, one way or another. "I promise, Sarah. I promise we'll find a way. I want to be with you. I'll figure things out with Emily and Max."

Sarah's tears spilled over, and she leaned in to kiss him, their lips meeting in a tender, emotional embrace. "Thank you, James. I need you to know how much this means to me."

James held her close, the warmth of her body providing a brief respite from the turmoil inside him. "I know, Sarah. I need you too. We'll make this work, somehow."

They spent the rest of the evening wrapped in each other's arms, the weight of their promise hanging over them. The future was uncertain, but for now, they found solace in their love and commitment to one another.

The next morning, they woke up entwined, the first rays of sunlight filtering through the curtains. James watched Sarah as she slept, her peaceful expression a stark contrast to the storm of emotions within him. He gently brushed a strand of hair from her face, his heart swelling with love and determination.

When Sarah stirred and opened her eyes, she smiled up at him. "Good morning, James."

"Good morning," he replied, leaning down to kiss her forehead. "I meant what I said last night, Sarah. We'll find a way."

Sarah nodded, her eyes shining with hope. "I believe you, James. I'm willing to fight for us, no matter what it takes."

James felt a renewed sense of purpose. He knew the road ahead would be difficult, but he was ready to face it with Sarah by his side. As they lay together, he silently vowed to find a way to balance his love for Sarah with his responsibilities to his family.

In the days that followed, James took steps to address the situation at home. He and Emily continued their counseling sessions, working to rebuild their fractured relationship. He spent more time with Max, making sure his son knew how much he was loved and supported.

But his heart remained with Sarah, and he cherished every moment they could steal away together. Their love grew stronger, fueled by their shared determination to create a future together.

One evening, as they sat on Sarah's balcony, watching the city lights twinkle below, James took her hand. "I've been thinking about our future, Sarah. I want to be with you, truly and completely. I'm going to talk to Emily. We need to figure out a way forward."

Sarah squeezed his hand, her eyes filled with love and gratitude. "Thank you, James. I know this isn't easy, but we'll get through it together."

James nodded, his resolve firm. "Yes, we will. No matter what, we'll find a way."

As they sat together, their hearts and hands entwined, they knew that their love was worth fighting for. The path ahead was uncertain, but they were ready to face it, together.

Chapter 13: Suspicions Confirmed

Emily stood in the dimly lit bedroom, her hands trembling as she held James' phone. She had found it buzzing on the kitchen counter, a message from Sarah lighting up the screen. Her heart pounded as she read the words, her mind reeling with the implications. The truth she had suspected for so long was now staring her in the face.

James walked into the room, still in his work clothes, his tie slightly askew. He froze when he saw Emily standing there, his phone in her hand, her face a mask of pain and anger.

"Emily, I can explain," he started, his voice shaky.

Emily looked up, her eyes filled with tears. "Explain? Explain what, James? That you've been lying to me? That you've been seeing someone else behind my back?"

James took a step forward, his heart heavy with guilt. "Please, Emily. Let's sit down and talk about this."

Emily's hands shook as she held up the phone, the message from Sarah still displayed. "How long, James? How long have you been lying to me?"

James sighed, his shoulders slumping. "It's been a few months."

Emily felt like the ground was falling out from under her. "A few months? And you didn't think to tell me? You just let me live in this lie?"

James reached out to her, but she stepped back, her eyes blazing with anger. "Emily, I didn't want to hurt you. I didn't know how to tell you."

Emily's voice rose, trembling with emotion. "You didn't know how to tell me? You didn't know how to be honest with your wife? Do you have any idea how humiliating this is?"

James felt tears prick his eyes. "I'm so sorry, Emily. I never wanted to hurt you. I've been so confused."

Emily's anger flared. "Confused? About what? About who you love? About where you belong?"

James looked down, his guilt overwhelming. "I love you, Emily. But things haven't been right between us for a long time."

Emily's voice broke, tears streaming down her face. "And you thought having an affair would fix that? You thought betraying me would somehow make things better?"

James shook his head, his own tears falling. "No, I was wrong. I was so wrong. But it wasn't just about that. It was about finding something I felt I'd lost."

Emily sat down on the edge of the bed, her strength waning. "What about us, James? What about our family? Did you even think about Max?"

James knelt in front of her, his heart breaking. "Every day, Emily. I think about you and Max every day. And I know I've messed up. I know I've hurt you."

Emily's voice was soft, filled with despair. "I don't know if I can ever trust you again, James. I don't know if we can come back from this."

James reached out, taking her hands in his. "Please, Emily. Let's try to fix this. For Max, for us. I'll do whatever it takes."

Emily looked into his eyes, searching for the truth. "I don't know, James. I don't know if I can forgive you."

James squeezed her hands, his voice pleading. "I'll do anything, Emily. Just give me a chance. Let's go to counseling, let's talk about it. Please."

The room was filled with the heavy silence of their shared pain. Emily looked away, her mind swirling with emotions. "I need time, James. I need to think."

James nodded, his heart heavy. "Take all the time you need. I'm not going anywhere. I'll wait for you."

Emily stood up, pulling her hands away. "I'm going to stay at my sister's for a while. I need some space."

James felt a wave of despair wash over him. "I understand. Just know that I love you, Emily. And I'm so sorry."

Emily walked to the door, her heart breaking with each step. "We'll see, James. We'll see."

As she left the room, James sat down on the bed, his head in his hands. The weight of his actions pressed down on him, the reality of his betrayal sinking in. He knew he had a long road ahead if he wanted to rebuild the trust he had shattered, and he was determined to do whatever it took to make things right.

Chapter 14: Comfort

James parked his car in a secluded corner of the parking lot, his heart racing. The sun had just set, and the dim glow of streetlights cast long shadows across the asphalt. He glanced at his phone, checking the time. Sarah would be here any minute. He adjusted his tie, the remnants of his workday still clinging to him. He felt a mixture of guilt and anticipation, the weight of his actions pressing down on him.

Sarah's car pulled up beside his, and she stepped out, wearing a light summer dress that fluttered in the evening breeze. Her auburn hair cascaded over her shoulders, catching the faint light. She looked around nervously, then smiled when she saw James. She quickly got into his car, and they embraced, the tension between them melting away.

"James," she whispered, her voice filled with longing. "I've missed you."

"I've missed you too, Sarah," he replied, holding her close. "I'm sorry for all of this. I'm trying to figure everything out."

Sarah looked up at him, her eyes reflecting her concern. "How are things at home? Did you talk to Emily?"

James sighed, running a hand through his hair. "Yes, we talked. It was awful. She found out everything. Max heard part of it. I don't know what to do."

Sarah reached out, cupping his face in her hands. "I'm so sorry, James. I hate seeing you go through this."

James closed his eyes, leaning into her touch. "I hate hurting everyone like this. But being with you feels right. It's the only time I feel like myself."

Sarah leaned in, kissing him gently. "I feel the same way, James. I wish things were different."

Their kiss deepened, the car becoming their temporary sanctuary. The world outside faded away, leaving only the two of them in their bubble of intimacy. The tension and pain of their lives seemed to dissipate, replaced by the warmth and comfort of their connection.

A sudden noise outside startled them. A passerby walked through the parking lot, glancing curiously at the car before moving on. James and Sarah pulled away, their hearts pounding.

"We have to be careful," Sarah whispered, her eyes wide with fear.

James nodded, his mind racing. "I know. But I can't stay away from you."

They sat in silence for a moment, the reality of their situation sinking in. The parking lot, once a place of refuge, now felt exposed and vulnerable. James reached out, taking Sarah's hand.

"Let's go somewhere else," he suggested. "Somewhere we can be alone."

Sarah nodded, her expression relieved. "Yes, let's do that."

They drove in silence, the tension between them replaced by a shared determination. James navigated the quiet streets, eventually finding a secluded spot by the lake. The water shimmered in the moonlight, the gentle lapping of waves providing a soothing backdrop.

They sat in the car, the cool night air filtering through the open windows. James reached over, taking Sarah's hand in his. "Thank you for being here, Sarah. I don't know what I'd do without you."

Sarah squeezed his hand, her eyes filled with love and concern. "You don't have to thank me, James. I'm here because I want to be. We'll figure this out together."

James leaned in, their foreheads touching. "I love you, Sarah."

"I love you too, James," she whispered, her voice filled with emotion.

They kissed again, the world outside their car forgotten. In each other's arms, they found a brief respite from the chaos of their lives. The future was uncertain, but for now, they had this moment, and it was enough.

As the night wore on, they talked about their dreams and fears, their hopes for a future where they could be together without hiding. They knew the road ahead would be difficult, but their love gave them the strength to face whatever challenges lay ahead.

The lake, with its calm and steady presence, seemed to promise a sense of peace and resolution. In the quiet of the night, James and Sarah held each other close, finding comfort and solace in their shared love. The journey was far from over, but together, they felt ready to face it, one step at a time.

Chapter 15: The Fallout

The house was filled with an unbearable tension. The air seemed thicker, the walls closer, every sound amplified in the heavy silence. Emily sat at the kitchen table, her hands trembling around a mug of cold coffee. She wore a simple sweater and jeans, her face pale and drawn. The morning light streamed through the window, casting long shadows that mirrored the turmoil in her heart.

James stood by the doorway, his expression a mix of guilt and sorrow. He was still in his work clothes, the tie loosened, his hair disheveled. He took a deep breath, trying to steady his voice. "Emily, we need to talk about this. We can't go on like this."

Emily looked up, her eyes red and swollen from crying. "Talk? What's there to talk about, James? You've betrayed me. You've betrayed us."

James stepped closer, his heart aching at the sight of her pain. "I know I've hurt you, Emily. I know I've made terrible mistakes. But I want to make things right. I want to fix this."

Emily's voice shook with anger and despair. "Fix this? How do you fix something that's broken beyond repair? How do you expect me to trust you again?"

Before James could respond, they heard the sound of footsteps. Max stood at the bottom of the stairs, his face pale, his eyes wide with fear and confusion. He was wearing his school uniform, his backpack slung over one shoulder.

"Mom? Dad? What's going on?" Max's voice trembled.

Emily wiped her tears, trying to compose herself. "Max, honey, go back to your room. We'll talk later."

Max shook his head, his voice rising. "No, I want to know. Are you two getting a divorce?"

James felt his heart drop, the weight of his son's words hitting him like a punch. "Max, it's complicated. Your mom and I are trying to work things out."

Max's eyes filled with tears. "Trying to work things out? I heard you arguing. I heard Mom crying. You've been lying to us, haven't you?"

Emily reached out to Max, her voice breaking. "Max, please, it's not that simple."

Max stepped back, his face contorted with anger and betrayal. "Not that simple? You've been lying to me! To both of us! How could you do this?"

James moved towards Max, his voice pleading. "Max, I'm so sorry. I never wanted to hurt you."

Max looked at his father, his eyes filled with hurt and confusion. "I trusted you. I looked up to you. And you've been lying this whole time."

Emily stood up, her body shaking with emotion. "Max, we're going to try to fix this. We're going to do everything we can to make things right."

Max shook his head, tears streaming down his face. "I don't believe you. I don't believe anything you say anymore."

He turned and ran up the stairs, the sound of his bedroom door slamming echoing through the house. Emily collapsed back into her chair, her sobs filling the room. James stood there, his heart breaking, feeling utterly helpless.

"Emily, I'm so sorry," James whispered, his voice choked with emotion. "I never wanted this to happen."

Emily looked up at him, her eyes filled with a mix of anger and sadness. "Sorry isn't enough, James. I don't know if I can ever forgive you."

James knelt beside her, his tears falling freely. "Please, Emily. Let's try to work through this. For Max, for us. I'll do whatever it takes."

Emily shook her head, her voice hollow. "I need time, James. I need time to think. I can't do this right now."

James nodded, his heart heavy with despair. "Take all the time you need. I'll be here. I'm not giving up on us."

The rest of the day passed in a blur of silence and tension. James tried to reach out to Max, but his son remained locked in his room, refusing to speak to him. Emily stayed in the kitchen, lost in her thoughts, her face a mask of pain.

As night fell, James found himself sitting alone in the living room, the weight of his actions pressing down on him. He knew the road ahead would be long and difficult, filled with uncertainty and pain. But he was determined to fight for his family, no matter what it took.

The household was in turmoil, the bonds of trust shattered, but James held onto the hope that they could find a way to heal. He knew it would take time, patience, and a lot of love, but he was ready to face the challenges ahead. For Emily, for Max, and for the future they had once dreamed of together.

Chapter 16: Heart-to-Heart

JAMES STOOD OUTSIDE Max's bedroom door, his heart heavy with dread. The house was eerily quiet, the only sound the faint ticking of the clock in the hallway. He took a deep breath, steeling himself for the conversation he knew he had to have. He knocked gently, his voice soft. "Max, can I come in?"

There was a long pause before Max's voice, thick with emotion, responded. "Yeah, I guess."

James opened the door and stepped inside. Max was sitting on his bed, his knees drawn up to his chest, his face pale and tear-streaked. The room was dimly lit, the curtains drawn, creating an atmosphere of isolation and sadness.

"Hey, buddy," James began, his voice trembling. "Can we talk?"

Max looked up, his eyes filled with hurt and betrayal. "What's there to talk about, Dad? You've already lied to me. To all of us."

James felt a pang of guilt and sorrow. He sat down on the edge of the bed, his heart aching at the sight of his son's pain. "I know, Max. I know I've let you down. And I'm so sorry. But I want to try to explain."

Max hugged his knees tighter, his voice shaking. "Explain what? That you've been cheating on Mom? That you've been lying to us for months?"

James swallowed hard, the words sticking in his throat. "Yes. I know it's hard to understand, but I never wanted to hurt you or your mom. I got lost, Max. I made terrible mistakes."

Max's eyes flashed with anger. "Lost? How could you get lost? We're your family. We're supposed to be enough."

James felt tears welling up in his eyes. "You are enough, Max. You and your mom mean everything to me. But sometimes, adults... we make mistakes. We get confused, and we do things we regret."

Max's voice rose, filled with anguish. "But why, Dad? Why did you have to do this? Why couldn't you just talk to Mom?"

James looked down, the weight of his actions pressing down on him. "I don't know, Max. I should have talked to her. I should have done a lot of things differently. But I can't change the past. All I can do now is try to make things right."

Max's eyes filled with tears. "How, Dad? How are you going to make this right?"

James reached out, placing a hand on Max's shoulder. "By being here for you. By being honest. By working hard to fix what I've broken. I know it won't be easy, and it will take time, but I'm not giving up on us."

Max shook his head, tears streaming down his face. "I don't know if I can trust you again. I don't know if things will ever be the same."

James felt his heart break at his son's words. "I understand, Max. And I'm willing to do whatever it takes to earn back your trust. I love you, son. More than anything."

Max looked at him, his expression a mix of hurt and longing. "I love you too, Dad. But it hurts so much."

James pulled Max into a tight embrace, his own tears falling freely. "I know it does, buddy. I know. And I'm so sorry. But we'll get through this together. I promise."

They sat there for a long time, holding each other, the weight of their emotions filling the room. The conversation had been painful and unresolved, but it was a start. A step towards healing the wounds that had been inflicted.

As the evening turned into night, James and Max talked about everything and nothing, their bond slowly beginning to mend. They knew the road ahead would be long and difficult, but for the first time in a long while, there was a glimmer of hope. A promise of better days to come, forged in the fires of their shared pain and love.

Chapter 17: A New Beginning

James packed his suitcase in silence, the weight of his decision pressing heavily on his shoulders. The dim light of the bedroom cast long shadows, emphasizing the emptiness he felt inside. He wore a simple shirt and jeans, his usual confident demeanor replaced by a weary resignation. Emily had agreed that a temporary separation might be best for everyone, giving them all some space to process the upheaval in their lives.

He took a deep breath, zipping up his suitcase and glancing around the room one last time. Memories of happier times flooded his mind, making his departure even more painful. He grabbed his keys and headed for the door, his heart aching as he heard Max's door open behind him.

"Dad?" Max's voice was small and filled with uncertainty.

James turned, his eyes meeting his son's. "Yeah, buddy?"

Max hesitated, tears welling up in his eyes. "Are you coming back?"

James knelt down, pulling Max into a tight embrace. "I promise, Max. This is just for a little while. I need to figure some things out, but I'm not leaving you. I'll always be here for you."

Max clung to him, his voice muffled. "I love you, Dad."

James's voice broke. "I love you too, Max. More than anything."

He stood up, giving Max one last reassuring smile before walking out the door. The drive to Sarah's place was filled with a mix of relief and guilt. He knew he needed this time to clear his head and make sense of his feelings, but leaving his family behind felt like a betrayal.

Sarah's apartment was a small, cozy space filled with warmth and light. She greeted him at the door, her eyes reflecting her concern and support. She wore a soft sweater and jeans, her hair pulled back in a casual ponytail.

"James," she said softly, pulling him into a comforting embrace. "I'm glad you're here."

James held her tightly, feeling some of the tension drain away. "Thanks, Sarah. I didn't know where else to go."

They moved to the living room, sitting close on the couch. Sarah handed him a cup of tea, the warmth seeping into his cold hands. "Tell me what happened."

James sighed, staring into the steaming cup. "Emily and I agreed that it would be best if I moved out for a while. Everything's such a mess right now. I need to figure out how to fix it."

Sarah reached out, placing a comforting hand on his arm. "You're doing the right thing, James. Sometimes space is what we need to see things clearly."

James looked at her, his eyes filled with a mix of gratitude and uncertainty. "I hope so. But it's so hard, Sarah. I feel like I'm failing everyone."

Sarah leaned in, her voice gentle but firm. "You're not failing, James. You're trying to make things right. That takes strength and courage."

They sat in silence for a while, the weight of their situation hanging in the air. Finally, Sarah spoke, her voice filled with quiet determination. "James, have you thought about what you really want? Not just for now, but for the future?"

James looked at her, his heart aching with the complexity of his emotions. "I want to be with you, Sarah. But I also want to be there for Max. I need to find a way to balance both."

Sarah nodded, her eyes reflecting her understanding. "We can make this work, James. It won't be easy, but we can find a way. We'll start a new life together, one step at a time."

James felt a glimmer of hope at her words. "Do you really think we can?"

Sarah smiled, her eyes shining with love and confidence. "I know we can. We'll face the challenges together, and we'll come out stronger on the other side."

James took her hand, holding it tightly. "Thank you, Sarah. I don't know what I'd do without you."

They spent the evening talking about their dreams and fears, their hopes for the future. The apartment, filled with the soft glow of lamplight, became a sanctuary of comfort and possibility. For the first time in a long while, James felt a sense of direction and purpose.

As the night wore on, they made plans for their new beginning. They talked about finding a place to live, blending their lives in a way that honored both their love and James's commitment to Max. The road ahead was uncertain, but together, they felt ready to face whatever came their way.

James knew there would be difficult conversations and painful decisions ahead, but with Sarah by his side, he felt stronger. They were building a future together, one step at a time, and that future, despite its challenges, was filled with hope and love.

Chapter 18: Reflection

Emily sat in the quiet of the living room, the house feeling emptier than ever. Max was at a friend's house, giving her a rare moment of solitude. She wore a simple blouse and jeans, her hair pulled back in a loose ponytail. Her eyes were red from crying, the weight of the past few weeks pressing heavily on her.

She picked up her phone and dialed a familiar number. "Hey, it's Emily. Can we talk? I really need someone to talk to."

Her close colleague, Mark, answered almost immediately. "Of course, Emily. Do you want to come over, or should I come to you?"

Emily hesitated, then decided. "I'll come over. I need to get out of the house."

Mark had been a part of her life for five years, ever since they started working together at the marketing firm. He was her confidant, her sounding board, and the one person who had always been there for her through thick and thin. They had shared countless late nights working on projects, laughing over coffee breaks, and supporting each other through personal struggles. Mark had always been steady, dependable, and kind—a true friend in every sense.

She drove to Mark's apartment, the city lights blurring as she tried to focus on the road. Mark had been a steady presence in her life for years, someone she trusted deeply. She needed his perspective, his comfort.

When she arrived, Mark opened the door, his expression filled with concern. He wore a casual shirt and jeans, his hair slightly tousled. "Emily, come in. You look exhausted."

Emily stepped inside, the warmth of his apartment a stark contrast to the cold emptiness she felt inside. "Thanks, Mark. I just... I don't know what to do anymore."

They sat on the couch, a cup of tea in Emily's hands. She looked around the room, taking in the familiar surroundings. "I feel like my whole life is falling apart. James is gone, and I don't know if I can ever forgive him. Max is struggling, and I don't know how to help him."

Mark listened, his eyes never leaving her face. "Emily, you've been through so much. It's okay to feel lost. But you're not alone. You have friends who care about you."

Emily's voice shook. "I keep thinking about my marriage, about what went wrong. Did I do something to push him away? Did I miss the signs?"

Mark reached out, taking her hand in his. "You can't blame yourself for his choices. You did the best you could. Sometimes people just drift apart."

Emily looked down at their intertwined hands, the touch sending a shiver through her. "I just don't know if I can keep going like this. I feel so alone."

Mark's voice was soft, filled with empathy. "You're not alone, Emily. I'm here for you. Always."

They sat in silence for a moment, the weight of their emotions filling the room. Emily looked up, her eyes meeting Mark's. "Thank you, Mark. For everything."

Mark leaned closer, his voice barely a whisper. "Emily, you mean a lot to me. More than you know."

Emily felt a rush of warmth, the loneliness inside her easing slightly. She leaned in, their lips meeting in a tender, hesitant kiss. The kiss deepened, their emotions pouring out in the intimate embrace.

Mark's hands moved to her waist, pulling her closer as their kiss grew more passionate. Emily responded, her fingers tangling in his hair. The warmth of his body against hers was a comforting balm to her aching heart. She felt herself melting into his touch, the tension of the past few weeks slowly dissipating.

They pulled back slightly, their foreheads touching, both breathing heavily. Emily's eyes filled with tears. "I'm sorry, Mark. I didn't mean for this to happen."

Mark shook his head, his expression gentle. "Don't apologize. We both needed this. But we need to talk about what it means."

Emily nodded, her heart heavy with conflicting emotions. "I know. I just... I'm so confused."

Mark took her hands in his, his voice steady. "We'll figure it out, Emily. Together. One step at a time."

They sat back on the couch, their bodies still close. Mark wrapped an arm around her shoulders, and Emily rested her head against his chest. The steady beat of his heart was a soothing rhythm that helped calm her racing thoughts.

As the night wore on, they talked about their dreams and fears, their hopes for the future. Emily found comfort in Mark's presence, a sense of safety she hadn't felt in a long time. Their connection deepened as they shared their vulnerabilities, and Emily began to see a glimmer of hope for the first time in weeks.

Later, as they moved to the bedroom, the intimacy between them grew. They undressed slowly, savoring the closeness and the comfort they found in each other. Mark's touch was gentle and reassuring, his kisses tender and filled with unspoken promises. Emily felt a sense of release, the burdens of her heart lightening as they held each other through the night.

The next morning, she woke up feeling a strange sense of peace. She looked over at Mark, still asleep beside her, and knew that whatever happened next, she had the strength to face it. She would take things one day at a time, focusing on what was best for her and Max.

Emily knew the road ahead would be challenging, but she felt ready to take the first steps toward a new beginning. With the support of friends like Mark, she believed she could find her way through the darkness and into the light of a brighter future.

Chapter 19: The Proposal

JAMES STOOD BY THE window of Sarah's apartment, looking out at the city lights twinkling in the distance. The room was softly lit, creating a warm and intimate atmosphere. He wore a simple button-down shirt and slacks, his hair slightly tousled from running his hands through it nervously. Sarah sat on the couch, her legs tucked under her, wearing a comfortable sweater and jeans. She watched him with a mixture of curiosity and concern.

"James, what's on your mind?" Sarah asked gently, her eyes searching his face.

James turned to face her, taking a deep breath. "Sarah, I've been thinking a lot about us, about our future."

Sarah's heart skipped a beat. She could see the seriousness in his eyes, the weight of his thoughts. "And?"

James walked over and sat beside her, taking her hands in his. "I love you, Sarah. I can't imagine my life without you. These past few months, despite all the turmoil, have shown me how much you mean to me."

Sarah's eyes softened, but she also felt a pang of worry. "I love you too, James. But you know it's not that simple."

James nodded, his grip on her hands tightening. "I know. But I've been thinking about how we can make this work. How we can build a life together. I want us to be together, openly and honestly. I want to start a new chapter with you."

Sarah looked down, her thoughts racing. She had dreamt of this moment, but now that it was here, she felt a mix of emotions. "James, what about Emily? What about Max? They're still a big part of your life. This isn't just about us."

James sighed, his heart heavy. "I know, Sarah. I've thought about them too. I don't want to hurt them any more than I already have. But I also can't keep living a lie. I need to be true to myself, and I need to be with you."

Sarah's eyes filled with tears. "I want that too, James. But I'm scared. What if things don't work out? What if this only causes more pain?"

James reached up, gently wiping away her tears. "We'll take it one step at a time. We'll face the challenges together. I'm willing to do whatever it takes to make this work. I believe in us, Sarah."

Sarah leaned into his touch, feeling the warmth and sincerity in his words. "I believe in us too, James. But I need time. Time to think, to make sure this is the right decision for everyone involved."

James nodded, understanding her hesitation. "Take all the time you need, Sarah. I'm not going anywhere. I'll be here, ready to build a future with you whenever you're ready."

They sat in silence for a moment, the gravity of their conversation sinking in. Sarah felt a flicker of hope, knowing that James was committed to making their relationship work. But she also knew that the path ahead would be fraught with complications and difficult decisions.

"James," Sarah began softly, "I want this too. But we need to be careful. We need to make sure we're not rushing into something without thinking it through."

James smiled, relief flooding his features. "I agree, Sarah. We'll take it slow, make sure we're doing what's best for everyone. But I'm willing to fight for us, for our future."

Sarah leaned in, their foreheads touching. "I'm willing to fight for us too."

They kissed, a gentle and tender connection that spoke volumes about their commitment to each other. The future was uncertain, but their love gave them the strength to face whatever challenges lay ahead.

As the night went on, they talked about their dreams and plans, imagining a life where they could be together without hiding. They knew it wouldn't be easy, but their love and determination gave them hope.

James felt a sense of peace he hadn't felt in a long time. He knew there would be difficult conversations with Emily and Max, and that the road to building a new life with Sarah would be long and complicated. But with Sarah by his side, he felt ready to face whatever came their way.

Sarah, too, felt a renewed sense of purpose. She knew that their journey was just beginning, and that they would need to navigate the complexities of their situation with care and compassion. But for the first time, she allowed herself to dream of a future where she and James could be truly happy together.

The proposal wasn't a traditional one, with rings and grand gestures, but it was filled with genuine emotion and a promise of a future built on love and honesty. As they held each other close, they both knew that they were embarking on a new and hopeful chapter in their lives.

Chapter 20: The Ultimatum

James stood in the hallway; his suitcase half-packed at his feet. The house felt strange and unfamiliar, the warmth of family life replaced by a cold, uneasy tension. He wore a simple shirt and jeans, his face drawn and tired. He glanced up as Emily entered the room, her expression guarded and resolute. She wore a comfortable sweater and jeans, her eyes red from crying.

"James, we need to talk," Emily said, her voice steady but laced with emotion.

James looked up, his heart sinking at the sight of her determined expression. "I know, Emily. I've been thinking about everything."

Emily took a deep breath, steeling herself for what she had to say. "This can't go on. I can't keep living like this, not knowing if you're coming or going, not knowing if we have a future. You need to make a choice."

James felt a wave of guilt and fear. "Emily, I—"

She cut him off, her voice rising. "No, James. No more excuses. It's either me and Max, or it's Sarah. But you can't have both."

James looked down at his hands, his mind racing. He loved Sarah, but the thought of losing his family was unbearable. "Emily, I don't want to lose you or Max. I'm trying to figure out what's best."

Emily's eyes filled with tears, her voice breaking. "What's best? What's best is for you to decide where your heart really lies. I deserve better than this. Max deserves better."

James stood up, his own eyes filled with unshed tears. "I know, Emily. I know I've hurt you. I never wanted this to happen."

Emily took a step closer, her anger and hurt boiling over. "Then why did it happen, James? Why did you let it get this far?"

James felt his heart breaking. "I got lost, Emily. I didn't know how to fix things between us. And Sarah... she made me feel alive again."

Emily's face twisted with pain. "And I don't? Our son doesn't? Is that what you're saying?"

James shook his head, his voice trembling. "No, that's not what I mean. I love you and Max more than anything. But things haven't been right between us for a long time."

Emily wiped her tears angrily. "So you thought having an affair would fix that? You thought betraying your family was the answer?"

James reached out, desperate to make her understand. "I made a terrible mistake. I know that. But I want to make things right. I want to try to fix this."

Emily pulled away, her eyes cold. "Then you need to end it with Sarah. Completely. If you want any chance of us rebuilding our lives, you need to show me that you're committed to this family."

James felt a wave of despair. "Emily, it's not that simple. I love Sarah too. I don't know if I can just walk away from her."

Emily's voice was cold and firm. "Then you've already made your choice. If you can't end it with her, then you need to leave. And don't expect it to be a clean break. This will be a messy divorce, and Max will know exactly why it's happening."

James felt like the ground was falling out from under him. "Emily, please. Don't do this. Give me some time to figure things out."

Emily shook her head, her voice final. "Time's up, James. You need to decide now. It's her or us."

The room fell silent, the weight of the ultimatum pressing down on both of them. James looked at Emily, seeing the pain and determination in her eyes. He knew she was serious, that there was no going back after this.

He took a deep breath, his heart aching with the enormity of the decision. "I need some air. I need to think."

Emily nodded, her eyes filled with unshed tears. "Take all the time you need, James. But when you come back, you better have an answer."

James walked out of the house, the cool night air hitting him like a wave. He felt torn apart, his heart pulled in two different directions. He loved Sarah, but he couldn't bear the thought of losing his family. The decision weighed heavily on him, and he knew that whatever choice he made, someone would be hurt.

Meanwhile, Emily felt a mix of anger, sadness, and relief. She had finally put her foot down, but the uncertainty of what James would decide weighed heavily on her. Her phone buzzed, pulling her out of her thoughts. It was Mark.

"Hey, Emily. How are you holding up?" Mark's voice was filled with concern.

"Not great, Mark. James is deciding whether to stay with us or leave for good." Emily's voice was strained.

"Do you want to come over? We can talk, or just sit in silence. Whatever you need." Mark's offer was genuine, and Emily felt a surge of gratitude.

"Okay, I'll come over. I need to get out of here." Emily grabbed her coat and left the house, her mind swirling with emotions.

When she arrived at Mark's apartment, he opened the door and pulled her into a comforting hug. "I'm glad you're here," he said softly.

Emily nodded, feeling a bit of the tension ease from her shoulders. They sat on the couch, and Mark handed her a glass of wine. "Tell me what happened," he urged gently.

Emily recounted the conversation with James, her voice shaking with emotion. Mark listened intently, his hand resting on her knee, providing a steady presence.

"I'm so sorry you're going through this, Emily. You deserve so much better," Mark said, his voice filled with sincerity.

Emily looked at him, tears in her eyes. "I don't know what to do, Mark. I'm so confused and hurt."

Mark leaned in, his voice soft. "You're stronger than you think, Emily. You'll get through this."

Emily felt a wave of gratitude and warmth toward Mark. She leaned in, and their lips met in a tender kiss. The kiss deepened, their emotions pouring out in the intimate embrace.

Mark's hands moved to her waist, pulling her closer as their kiss grew more passionate. Emily responded, her fingers tangling in his hair. The warmth of his body against hers was a comforting balm to her aching heart. She felt herself melting into his touch, the tension of the past few weeks slowly dissipating.

As their intimacy grew, Mark's demeanor changed. He became more aggressive, his touch firmer, his kisses more demanding. Emily found herself caught up in the intensity, her own emotions swirling in response. But as the moments passed, she began to feel a sense of discomfort.

Mark whispered harshly, "You like this, don't you? Being used?"

Emily felt a pang of unease. "Mark, please..."

He didn't seem to hear her, his actions growing more insistent. "You're mine tonight, Emily. Just like this."

Emily's initial thrill began to turn into apprehension. "Mark, stop. This isn't right."

Mark's grip tightened. "You wanted this. Don't pretend you didn't."

Emily's heart pounded, her discomfort turning to fear. "Mark, enough. Stop it."

Mark finally pulled back, his eyes wild. "What's wrong? You were enjoying it."

Emily shook her head, tears streaming down her face. "Not like this, Mark. Not like this."

Mark's face softened, regret flashing in his eyes. "I'm sorry, Emily. I got carried away."

Emily stood up, pulling her clothes back on. "This was a mistake. We can't do this again."

Mark reached out, but she stepped back. "Emily, please. I didn't mean to hurt you."

Emily's voice was cold and final. "I need to go. This isn't what I need right now."

As she left Mark's apartment, she felt a surge of determination. The encounter had shown her that she needed to take control of her life, to make decisions that were best for her and Max. She drove home, her mind clearer, her resolve stronger.

When she walked back into the house, she found James sitting on the couch, his face a mask of anguish. He looked up as she entered, his eyes filled with sorrow.

"Emily, I've made my decision," he said, his voice trembling. "I'm going to end it with Sarah. I want to try to fix things with you and Max."

Emily's eyes filled with tears, a mixture of relief and pain. "Thank you, James. It's going to be a long road, but we'll take it one step at a time."

James nodded, feeling a glimmer of hope. "I know. And I'm ready to do whatever it takes to make things right."

The journey ahead would be difficult, but for the first time, they were facing it together. And that, Emily hoped, would be enough to start healing the wounds they had inflicted on each other.

Chapter 21: Torn Between Worlds

James sat at the kitchen table, his head in his hands. The morning light streamed through the window, casting a harsh glare on the coffee cup in front of him. He wore a simple t-shirt and jeans, the casual clothes a stark contrast to the turmoil inside him. The house was quiet, but the silence was filled with the weight of his thoughts.

Max entered the room, his school uniform slightly rumpled. He paused when he saw his father, his young face filled with concern. "Dad? Are you okay?"

James looked up, forcing a smile. "Hey, buddy. Just thinking about some stuff. How about some breakfast?"

Max nodded, sitting down at the table. "Sure. Are you... are you staying home today?"

James felt a pang of guilt. "Yeah, I am. I needed a day to think."

Max's eyes searched his father's face. "Is it about Mom? And... everything?"

James sighed, reaching out to ruffle Max's hair. "Yeah, it is. But I promise, no matter what happens, I'm here for you. Okay?"

Max nodded, but his eyes were filled with worry. "I know, Dad. I just want things to be normal again."

James's heart ached at his son's words. "Me too, Max. Me too."

Later that day, James found himself standing outside Sarah's apartment. He took a deep breath before knocking on the door. When Sarah opened it, her face lit up with a smile, but it quickly faded when she saw the expression on his face.

"James? What's wrong?" she asked, stepping aside to let him in.

James entered, his heart heavy. "I needed to talk to you. About everything."

Sarah closed the door, turning to face him. She wore a simple dress, her hair falling loosely around her shoulders. "Okay. Let's sit down."

They sat on the couch, the familiarity of the setting doing little to ease the tension. James took Sarah's hand, his voice trembling. "Sarah, I love you. You know that. But I'm so torn right now. I feel like I'm being pulled in two different directions."

Sarah's eyes filled with concern. "I know, James. And I don't want to make things harder for you. But I need to know where we stand. What do you want?"

James looked down, his thoughts racing. "I want to be with you, Sarah. But I also have a responsibility to Max. He needs me, especially now."

Sarah nodded, her voice soft. "I understand that, James. But what about us? Can you really walk away from what we have?"

James felt tears prick his eyes. "I don't want to. But I don't know how to make it all work. I don't want to hurt anyone."

Sarah squeezed his hand, her eyes pleading. "I love you, James. And I want to be with you. But you need to make a choice. You can't keep living in this limbo."

James nodded, his heart heavy. "I know. And I promise I'll make a decision soon. I just need a little more time."

Sarah leaned in, kissing him softly. "I'm here for you, James. Whatever you decide, I'll support you."

James held her close, the warmth of her embrace a brief respite from the turmoil inside him. "Thank you, Sarah. I don't know what I'd do without you."

That evening, James returned home to find Max waiting for him. They sat together in the living room, the weight of the day pressing down on them.

"Dad, can we talk?" Max asked, his voice hesitant.

James nodded, turning to face his son. "Of course, Max. What's on your mind?"

Max took a deep breath. "I heard you and Mom talking. About the divorce. Are you really going to leave us?"

James felt a surge of guilt. "Max, I don't want to leave you. I love you and your mom very much. But things have been really hard lately."

Max's eyes filled with tears. "I don't want you to go, Dad. I don't want our family to break apart."

James pulled Max into a tight hug, his own tears falling freely. "I don't want that either, buddy. I'm trying to figure out what's best for all of us."

They sat in silence for a while, the weight of their emotions hanging heavy in the air. James knew he had to make a decision soon, but the path ahead seemed so unclear.

As the night wore on, James found himself alone in the living room, staring at the family photos on the wall. He thought about the life he had built with Emily and Max, the memories they had shared. He also thought about Sarah, the love and passion they had found together.

He knew that no matter what decision he made, someone would be hurt. But he also knew that he couldn't keep living in this state of limbo. He needed to find a way to move forward, for himself and for those he loved.

The next morning, James woke up with a sense of resolve. He knew the path ahead would be difficult, but he was ready to face it. He was ready to make the hard choices and to do whatever it took to build a future where he could be true to himself and to those he loved.

He just hoped that, in the end, it would be enough.

Chapter 22: The Decision

James sat alone in his car, parked on a quiet street a few blocks from home. The late afternoon sun cast long shadows, the fading light mirroring the turmoil in his heart. He wore a simple shirt and jeans, the same clothes he'd been in since leaving work. He stared at his phone, the screen displaying a text from Sarah asking how he was doing. He sighed, knowing the decision he faced would change everything.

He drove home slowly, his mind racing with memories and emotions. The house came into view, a place of comfort and conflict. He parked in the driveway and took a deep breath, steeling himself for what was to come. He stepped inside, the familiar sounds and smells wrapping around him like a blanket.

Emily was in the kitchen, preparing dinner. She wore a simple blouse and jeans, her face lined with worry and exhaustion. Max was at the table, working on his homework, his expression a mix of concentration and underlying anxiety.

"Hi," James said softly, stepping into the room.

Emily looked up, her eyes guarded. "Hi. Dinner will be ready soon."

Max glanced at his father, his eyes filled with questions he was too afraid to ask. James felt a pang of guilt, knowing how much his son had been affected by the tension in their home.

"Can we talk?" James asked, his voice trembling slightly.

Emily nodded, wiping her hands on a towel. "Max, could you give us a minute?"

Max gathered his books and left the room, his footsteps echoing down the hallway. Emily turned to face James, her arms crossed, her expression a mix of hope and dread.

"What is it, James?" she asked, her voice steady but filled with emotion.

James took a deep breath, meeting her gaze. "I've made a decision, Emily. About us, about Sarah."

Emily's eyes widened slightly, her heart pounding. "And?"

James looked down, his voice breaking. "I want to end it with Sarah. I want to try to fix things with you and Max. I know it won't be easy, but I'm willing to do whatever it takes."

Emily's eyes filled with tears, a mixture of relief and pain. "Are you sure, James? This isn't something you can go back on."

James nodded, his own tears welling up. "I'm sure, Emily. I love you and Max more than anything. I don't want to lose our family."

Emily stepped closer, her voice trembling. "It's going to be a long road, James. There's a lot of hurt to heal."

James reached out, taking her hands in his. "I know. And I'm ready to do whatever it takes. I want us to be a family again."

They stood there in silence, the weight of their decision pressing down on them. The air was heavy with emotion, the future uncertain but filled with a glimmer of hope.

Meanwhile, Sarah sat in her apartment, her phone in her hand, waiting for a response from James. She wore a simple dress, her hair pulled back, her expression one of quiet resignation. The waiting was agony, the uncertainty tearing at her heart.

Her phone buzzed, and she glanced at the screen. It was a message from James. She took a deep breath and opened it, her heart pounding.

"Sarah, we need to talk. Can I come over?"

She felt a wave of anxiety and relief, quickly typing a response. "Yes, come over."

James arrived at Sarah's apartment a short while later, his heart heavy with the conversation to come. He knocked softly, and Sarah opened the door, her eyes filled with concern and love.

"James," she said softly, stepping aside to let him in.

He walked in, the familiar surroundings filling him with a sense of comfort and sorrow. They sat on the couch, a palpable tension hanging in the air.

"Sarah, I've made a decision," James began, his voice trembling. "I need to end this. I need to try to fix things with my family."

Sarah's eyes filled with tears, her heart breaking. "I understand, James. I always knew this could happen."

James reached out, taking her hand. "I'm so sorry, Sarah. I never wanted to hurt you. You mean so much to me."

Sarah nodded, tears spilling down her cheeks. "I know, James. And I love you. But I understand. You need to do what's right for your family."

They sat in silence, holding hands, the weight of their parting pressing down on them. It was a bittersweet moment, filled with love and regret.

Back at home, Emily sat with Max, explaining the situation as best she could. Max listened, his eyes wide with confusion and relief.

"So, Dad's staying?" Max asked, his voice trembling.

Emily nodded, her eyes filled with tears. "Yes, Max. We're going to try to make things right."

Max hugged his mother tightly, a sense of hope filling his heart. "I'm glad, Mom. I missed him."

Emily held her son close, feeling the first glimmer of hope she had felt in weeks. The road ahead would be long and difficult, but for the first time, they were facing it together, as a family.

As James drove back home from Sarah's apartment, he felt a mixture of relief and sorrow. The decision had been made, and now it was time to focus on healing the wounds and rebuilding the trust that had been shattered.

When he walked through the door, Emily and Max were waiting. James took a deep breath, feeling the weight of his commitment settle into place.

"I'm home," he said softly, his eyes meeting Emily's.

"Welcome home," Emily replied, a tentative smile on her lips.

Max ran to his father, hugging him tightly. "I'm glad you're back, Dad."

James held his son close, feeling the warmth of his family's love surround him. It was a new beginning, filled with challenges and uncertainties, but also with the promise of healing and hope. Together, they would face whatever came next, one step at a time.

Chapter 23: The Aftermath

The air in the house felt lighter, but the wounds were still fresh. Emily and Max sat together on the couch, the warmth of their reunion providing a small comfort against the lingering tension. Emily wore a simple sweater and jeans, her face showing the strain of the past weeks but also a glimmer of hope. Max, in his school uniform, clung to her, his eyes filled with relief and love.

James entered the room, looking tentative but determined. He had changed into more comfortable clothes, trying to shed the weight of his recent decisions. "How are you both doing?" he asked softly.

Emily smiled weakly. "We're getting there, James. It's going to take time, but we'll make it."

Max looked up at his father. "I'm glad you're back, Dad. I missed you."

James felt a lump in his throat. "I missed you too, Max. More than you know."

They spent the evening talking about mundane things—school, work, plans for the weekend—trying to regain a sense of normalcy. But the underlying tension was palpable. They all knew the real work had just begun.

Later that night, after Max had gone to bed, Emily and James sat together in the living room, the dim light casting long shadows. Emily took a deep breath, her voice trembling. "James, there's something I need to tell you."

James turned to her, his heart pounding. "What is it, Emily?"

Emily looked down at her hands, her voice barely above a whisper. "While you were away, I... I went to see Mark."

James felt a cold knot of dread in his stomach. "What happened?"

Emily's eyes filled with tears. "I was so lost, James. I didn't know what to do. Mark has always been there for me, and I needed someone. We ended up... being intimate. It happened more than once."

James's heart sank. "Emily..."

She wiped her tears, her voice shaking. "The last time, it was different. He was different. He was aggressive, and it made me uncomfortable. I realized then that I was making a mistake. I told him we couldn't do it anymore, but I didn't tell you because I didn't want to hurt you more."

James felt a mix of anger, hurt, and sorrow. "Emily, why didn't you tell me?"

Emily's voice broke. "I was scared, James. Scared of losing you, scared of what it meant for us. I was trying to find something to hold onto, and I made a terrible mistake."

James took a deep breath, trying to process the information. "Does he know it's over?"

Emily nodded. "Yes, he called me again today, but I didn't answer. I know I need to tell him firmly that it's really over."

James reached out, taking her hand. "Emily, I know we both made mistakes. But we have to be honest with each other if we're going to make this work. No more secrets."

Emily squeezed his hand, her eyes filled with determination. "I promise, James. No more secrets."

The next morning, as James prepared breakfast, his phone buzzed with a message from Sarah. He felt a pang of guilt but knew he needed to address it. "Emily, I need to call Sarah. I need to end things properly."

Emily nodded, her face composed but understanding. "Do what you need to do, James."

James stepped outside, the cool morning air hitting his face. He dialed Sarah's number, his heart heavy. She answered after the first ring. "James?"

"Sarah, we need to talk," he said, his voice steady but filled with sorrow.

Sarah's voice was calm, though he could hear the pain behind it. "I figured. What's going on?"

James took a deep breath. "I'm going to try to fix things with Emily and Max. I can't continue our relationship. It's not fair to anyone involved."

There was a long pause. "I understand, James. I always knew this could happen. I just hoped..."

"I know, Sarah. I'm so sorry for everything. You mean a lot to me, but I have to do what's right for my family."

Sarah's voice was barely a whisper. "I get it, James. I hope you find the happiness you're looking for."

James hung up, feeling a weight lift off his shoulders but also a deep sense of loss. He walked back inside, where Emily was waiting with a cup of coffee. She handed it to him, her eyes searching his face.

"How did it go?" she asked.

James sighed, taking a sip. "It was hard, but it needed to be done. She understands."

Emily nodded, her face reflecting her own mixture of relief and sorrow. "We'll get through this, James. Together."

The days turned into weeks, and slowly, the family began to heal. James and Emily attended counseling sessions, working through their pain and rebuilding their trust. Max, seeing the effort his parents were making, began to open up more, his smile returning.

One evening, as they sat together watching a movie, Emily's phone buzzed. She glanced at the screen and saw it was Mark. She felt a pang of anxiety but knew what she had to do.

"James, it's Mark. I need to take this."

James nodded, his eyes filled with support. "Go ahead."

Emily stepped outside, taking a deep breath before answering. "Mark, we need to talk."

Mark's voice was tense. "Emily, I've been trying to reach you. We need to see each other."

Emily's voice was firm. "No, Mark. We don't. What happened between us was a mistake, and it's over. I need to focus on my family."

There was a long silence. "I see. I'm sorry if I hurt you, Emily. I didn't mean to."

Emily felt a wave of sadness but also a sense of closure. "I know, Mark. But this is how it has to be. Goodbye."

She hung up, feeling a sense of finality. She walked back inside, where James and Max were waiting. She sat down beside James, taking his hand.

"It's done," she said softly. "No more secrets."

James kissed her forehead, his heart filled with love and determination. "No more secrets. We're in this together."

As the weeks turned into months, the family continued to heal, facing each challenge with honesty and love. The road was long and difficult, but together, they found the strength to move forward, one step at a time.

Chapter 24: Healing Wounds

James woke up early, the first light of dawn filtering through the curtains. He lay in bed for a moment, listening to the soft breathing of Emily beside him. She wore a simple nightgown, her face relaxed in sleep. James felt a surge of gratitude, knowing how far they had come. He gently got out of bed, careful not to wake her, and headed downstairs to start breakfast.

In the kitchen, he began preparing pancakes, the familiar routine soothing. The smell of coffee and sizzling batter filled the air. Max soon joined him, still in his pajamas, his hair tousled from sleep.

"Morning, Dad," Max said, rubbing his eyes.

"Morning, buddy," James replied, ruffling his son's hair. "How about some pancakes?"

Max grinned. "Sounds good."

As they ate breakfast together, Emily came downstairs, a soft smile on her face. She wore a comfortable robe, her hair loosely tied back. She kissed James on the cheek before sitting down next to Max.

"Morning," she said, her voice warm.

"Morning, Mom," Max replied, his mouth full of pancakes.

James and Emily shared a look, a silent acknowledgment of the progress they had made. It wasn't perfect, but it was better. They were healing.

Later that day, James went to his counseling session. Dr. Harris, a middle-aged woman with kind eyes and a calming presence, welcomed him into her office.

"How have things been, James?" she asked, her voice gentle.

James took a deep breath. "Better. Emily and I are talking more, and Max seems happier. It's been hard, but we're getting there."

Dr. Harris nodded. "That's good to hear. Remember, healing takes time. Be patient with yourself and with them."

James nodded, feeling a sense of relief. "Thank you. I will."

Meanwhile, Emily felt a growing sense of responsibility to ensure that Sarah could find her own path to healing. Emily understood the complexity of the situation and the depth of emotions involved, but she also knew that setting clear boundaries was crucial for everyone's well-being. Determined to make things right, she decided to visit Sarah, hoping to foster a sense of normalcy and mutual understanding.

The next afternoon, Emily found herself standing at Sarah's door, feeling a mix of apprehension and resolve. She wore a casual dress, her demeanor calm and composed. When Sarah opened the door, her surprise quickly turned to a welcoming smile.

"Emily, it's good to see you," Sarah said, stepping aside to let her in.

"Thanks, Sarah. I hope I'm not intruding," Emily replied, her voice steady but warm.

"Not at all. Please, come in," Sarah assured her, leading Emily to the living room.

They sat down on the couch, the same place where their previous encounter had taken an unexpected turn. The room was filled with soft light, the late afternoon sun casting a warm glow through the windows.

"Sarah, I've been thinking a lot about what happened between you both," Emily began, choosing her words carefully. "I value the connection we have, but I also believe that what happened should not repeat. It's best for everyone if we set clear boundaries."

Sarah nodded, her expression thoughtful. "I understand, Emily. It was a moment of vulnerability for both of us, but I agree that we need to focus on healing and moving forward in a healthy way."

Emily felt a wave of relief wash over her. "I'm glad you understand. I care about James and you, Sarah, and I want us to be able to support each other without crossing any lines."

Sarah reached out and took Emily's hand, her eyes filled with sincerity. "I appreciate your honesty, Emily. I want the same. We've both been through so much, and it's important that we take care of ourselves and each other."

They spent the next hour talking about their lives, their struggles, and their hopes for the future. The conversation flowed easily, the bond between them growing stronger. Emily felt a sense of peace, knowing that they could navigate this difficult situation together as friends.

As the sun began to set, casting a beautiful array of colors across the sky, Emily stood to leave. "Thank you for understanding, Sarah. I feel like we're on the right path."

Sarah smiled, hugging Emily tightly. "Thank you for coming, Emily. I'm glad we had this talk. Let's keep supporting each other."

Over the next few weeks, Emily and Sarah continued to build their friendship. They met for coffee, shared stories about their lives, and offered each other encouragement and support. Their bond deepened as two women who had found a way to navigate their complicated emotions and emerge stronger.

Emily felt a renewed sense of purpose. She was committed to making her family whole again, but she also found solace in her friendship with Sarah. They both understood the importance of boundaries and the value of having someone to lean on.

One evening, as Emily and James sat on their porch watching the stars, she felt a profound sense of contentment. Max was doing well, and their family was healing. She glanced at James, who was gazing at the night sky.

"James, I'm so grateful for where we are now," Emily said softly, taking his hand.

James squeezed her hand gently. "Me too, Emily. We've come a long way, and I'm thankful for every step we've taken together."

Meanwhile, Sarah found her own path to happiness. She focused on her career, explored new hobbies, and cherished her friendship with Emily. They often laughed about their shared experiences, finding strength in their connection. How far will it go?

Chapter 25: A New Dawn

James had to attend an office conference, and Max was away for a boy scouts camp, leaving Emily alone that Friday and Saturday. Feeling a sense of excitement and anticipation, she decided to visit Sarah. As she drove to Sarah's apartment, the autumn leaves fell in a colorful cascade around her, adding to her sense of renewal and hope.

When Emily arrived at Sarah's apartment, she took a deep breath and rang the doorbell. The door opened, revealing Sarah with a warm, welcoming smile. Sarah was wearing a comfortable yet stylish outfit that perfectly suited the relaxed, intimate atmosphere of the evening. She had on a soft, light blue sweater that complemented her eyes and a pair of well-fitted dark jeans. Her hair was pulled back into a casual, loose bun, with a few wisps framing her face. She looked both effortlessly elegant and approachable, embodying the warmth and hospitality that made her home feel so inviting.

"Emily, it's so good to see you," Sarah said, stepping aside to let her in.

"Hi, Sarah. I hope I'm not intruding," Emily replied, her voice tinged with excitement and a hint of nervousness.

"Not at all. Come in, make yourself at home," Sarah assured her, leading Emily into the cozy living room.

The room was filled with soft light from the late afternoon sun, casting a warm, golden glow through the large windows. The comfortable furniture and personal touches around the room made it feel inviting and intimate. Emily noticed a vase of fresh flowers on the coffee table, their vibrant colors adding to the warmth of the space.

Sarah gestured to the couch, and Emily sat down, feeling the plush cushions envelop her. "Would you like a glass of wine?" Sarah asked, her voice friendly and accommodating.

"That sounds perfect," Emily replied, relaxing into the comfort of the setting.

As Sarah uncorked a bottle of red wine and poured it on each a glass, Emily looked around the room, appreciating the sense of peace it radiated. There were photos on the mantelpiece, bookshelves filled with an eclectic collection of novels and memoirs, and a soft throw blanket draped over the arm of the couch. Everything about the apartment spoke of Sarah's personality and her ability to create a welcoming atmosphere.

Sarah returned with the glasses of wine, the deep red liquid catching the light. She handed one to Emily and took a seat beside her on the couch. "To new beginnings," Sarah said, raising her glass.

"To new beginnings," Emily echoed, clinking her glass against Sarah's. They both took a sip, savoring the rich, velvety taste of the wine.

The conversation flowed easily as they discussed their lives, their dreams, and the challenges they had faced. The warmth of the wine and the intimacy of the setting made Emily feel more connected to Sarah than ever before. They laughed and shared stories, finding common ground in their experiences and perspectives.

Emily and Sarah's conversation flowed effortlessly as they moved from the living room to the kitchen. They prepared dinner together, the act of cooking providing a comforting rhythm. Emily wore a casual dress, while Sarah had changed into a comfortable sweater and jeans. The tension from earlier had dissipated, replaced by a growing sense of connection and intimacy.

As they finished their meal and moved back to the living room, the sun began to set, casting a warm glow through the windows. The light created a soft, intimate atmosphere, and Sarah poured them each another glass of wine. They settled on the couch, their conversation turning deeper and more personal.

"You know, Emily," Sarah began, her voice soft, "I've always admired your strength and resilience. Even when things were at their worst, you never gave up."

Emily looked at Sarah, feeling a warmth spread through her chest. "I never thought I was that strong. I just did what I had to do."

Sarah moved closer, her eyes searching Emily's face. "You are strong. And you've been through so much. It's incredible how you've managed to hold everything together."

Emily felt her heart quicken at Sarah's words and the intensity in her gaze. "Sarah, thank you. That means a lot."

Before she could say more, Sarah leaned in and kissed her softly. The kiss was tentative, filled with a mix of emotions. Emily felt a rush of confusion and desire, her mind racing. She pulled back slightly, her breath shaky.

"Sarah, what are we doing?" Emily whispered, her voice trembling.

Sarah looked into her eyes, her own emotions raw and visible. "I don't know, Emily. But this feels right. Doesn't it?"

Emily hesitated, then nodded slowly. "Yes, it does."

They kissed again, the intensity growing, their emotions pouring out in the intimate embrace. Wine was acting as an aphrodisiac. Emily felt Sarah's hands gently caress her back, pulling her closer. The warmth of Sarah's body against hers was a comforting balm to her aching heart. They moved together, exploring the new and unexpected connection between them.

Sarah led Emily to the bedroom, the atmosphere charged with anticipation. The soft glow of the bedside lamp bathed the room in a warm light, casting gentle shadows. They undressed slowly, savoring the closeness and the comfort they found in each other. Sarah's touch was gentle and reassuring, her kisses tender and filled with unspoken promises.

Emily felt a sense of release, the burdens of her heart lightening as they held each other. The intimacy was a revelation, a moment of pure connection and understanding. They moved together in a rhythm that felt natural and right, their bodies communicating the emotions they couldn't put into words.

Hours later, they lay in each other's arms, the room filled with the soft sounds of their breathing. Emily's mind was a whirlwind of thoughts and emotions. She felt a deep connection with Sarah, something unexpected but undeniably real.

As she dressed to leave, Sarah watched her, a look of understanding and concern on her face. "Emily, what happens now?"

Emily sighed, her heart heavy with uncertainty. "I don't know, Sarah. I need to figure things out. But this... this meant something to me."

Sarah nodded, her eyes reflecting her own uncertainty. "It meant something to me too."

Emily left Sarah's apartment Saturday morning, her mind racing with the implications of what had happened. She drove home, the streets blurring as she tried to make sense of her feelings. When she arrived, James and Max were waiting for her, their faces filled with concern.

"Emily, are you okay?" James asked, his voice filled with worry.

Emily took a deep breath, trying to steady herself. "I'm fine, James. Just tired, I think. I was out with my girlfriends and stayed with Kelsi."

Max hugged her tightly, his eyes filled with love. "We were worried about you, Mom."

Emily smiled, hugging him back. "I'm here now, Max. Everything's going to be okay."

As the family settled in for the night, Emily's mind continued to race. She knew she needed to talk to James, to be honest about what had happened. But for now, she focused on the love and support of her family, finding comfort in their presence. She never felt erogenous pleasure ever before like she had with Sarah. It was something beyond Emily's wildest imaginations. She thought it was no wonder James was so much into Sarah.

Emily's journey was far from over, and the path forward held many uncertainties. As she stood on the porch, watching the sun rise and touching her body, she felt a mix of hope and apprehension, knowing that the next chapter of her life was just beginning.

To be continued.

About the Author

Ivap Lawarga is a prolific author whose works explore the intricate dynamics of human relationships, resilience, and personal growth. With a background in psychology and a keen understanding of the human spirit, Ivap weaves narratives that resonate deeply with readers, offering insights into the complexities of love, forgiveness, and the paths to healing.

Born and raised in a small town, Ivap developed a passion for storytelling at an early age, finding inspiration in the everyday lives of people around him. This keen observation of human behavior and emotions has become a hallmark of his writing, bringing characters to life in a way that feels both authentic and relatable.